"Do you like him?" little Dylan asked his mom

"Who?" Laura asked, startled.

"Brandon Marsh."

"Yes, of course," she said quickly. What else could she say? How could she not like the handsome, brooding man who, in spite of himself, was being so good to her son?

"He likes you."

She flushed. She wanted to ask how Dylan knew that, but she didn't.

"He hasn't got a wife or a kid," Dylan continued. "We haven't got a dad." He paused and looked her in the eye.

Oh, Lord, Laura worried. How long would it take for her fatherless little boy to put two and two together...and start dreaming some impossible dream?

Dear Reader,

Welcome to another joy-filled month of heart, home and happiness from Harlequin American Romance! We're pleased to bring you four new stories filled with people you'll always remember and romance you'll never forget.

We've got more excitement for you this month as MAITLAND MATERNITY continues with Jacqueline Diamond's *I Do! I Do!* An elusive bachelor marries a lovely nurse for the sake of his twin nieces—will love turn their house into a home? Watch for twelve new books in this heartwarming series, starting next month from Harlequin Books!

How does a proper preacher's daughter tame the wildest man in the county? With a little help from a few Montana matchmakers determined to repopulate their town! Sparks are sure to fly in *The Playboy's Own Miss Prim*, the latest BACHELORS OF SHOTGUN RIDGE story by Mindy Neff!

An expectant mother, blinded from an accident, learns that the heart recognizes what the eye cannot see in Lisa Bingham's touching novel *Man Behind the Voice*. And when a little boy refuses to leave his ranch home, his mother must make a deal with the brooding, sexy new owner. Don't miss Carol Grace's delightful *Family Tree*.

Spice up your summer days with the best of Harlequin American Romance!

Warm wishes,

Melissa Jeglinski
Associate Senior Editor

Family Tree

CAROL GRACE

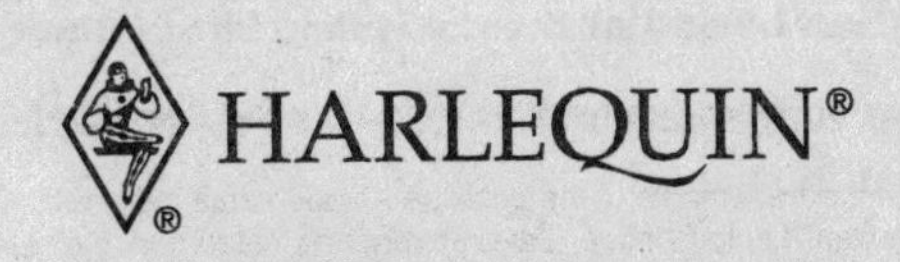

TORONTO • NEW YORK • LONDON
AMSTERDAM • PARIS • SYDNEY • HAMBURG
STOCKHOLM • ATHENS • TOKYO • MILAN • MADRID
PRAGUE • WARSAW • BUDAPEST • AUCKLAND

To my father, Roy Krueger (1907-1999).
The world's best dad.

ISBN 0-373-16836-5

FAMILY TREE

This edition published by arrangement with Harlequin Books S.A.

Visit us at www.eHarlequin.com

Printed in U.S.A.

ABOUT THE AUTHOR

Carol Grace has always been interested in travel and living abroad. She spent her junior year of college in France and toured the world, working on the hospital ship HOPE. She and her husband spent the first year and a half of their marriage in Iran, where they both taught English. Then, with their toddler daughter, they lived in Algeria for two years. For Carol, writing is another way of making her life exciting. Her office is her mountaintop home, which overlooks the Pacific Ocean. She lives there with her inventor husband, their daughter, who just graduated from college, and their teenage son. Carol has written over fifteen romances for Silhouette Books. This is her first Harlequin American Romance novel.

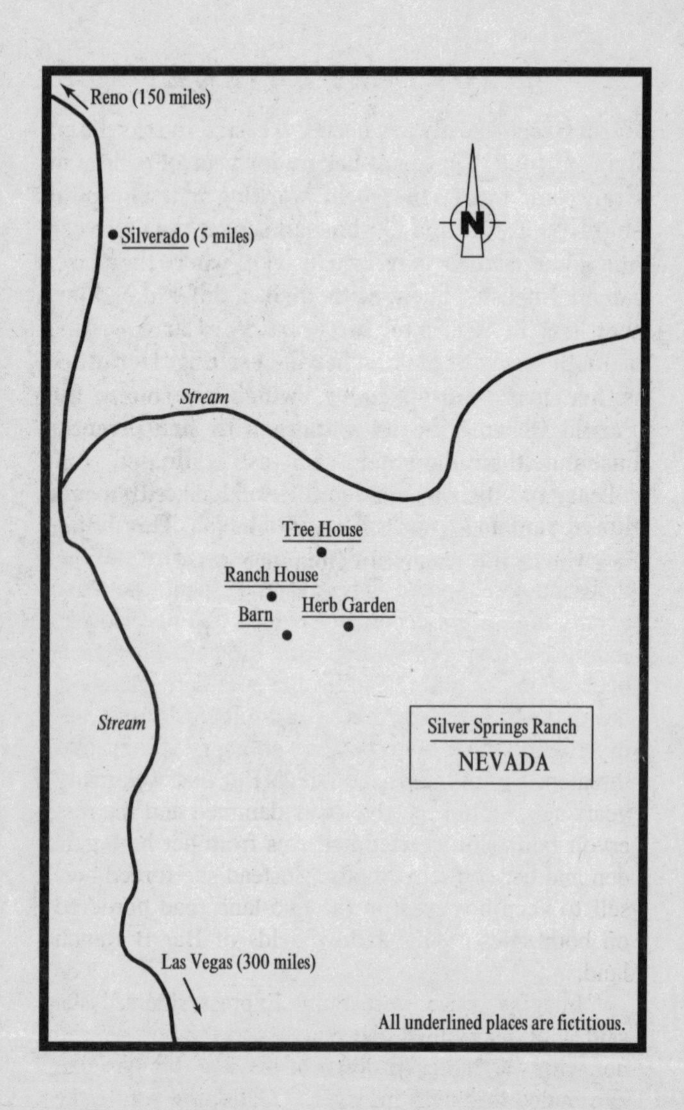
Reno (150 miles)
Silverado (5 miles)
N
Stream
Tree House
Ranch House
Herb Garden
Barn
Stream
Silver Springs Ranch
NEVADA
Las Vegas (300 miles)
All underlined places are fictitious.

Chapter One

''Don't look back,'' Laura warned her son as he craned his neck around for a last look at the ranch where he'd spent all eight years of his life.

Easy to say, but so difficult to do. Laura swallowed hard and followed her own advice. She didn't allow herself a last look in the rearview mirror at the thousand-acre spread where she'd spent the past twenty-nine years of her life, which had been in her family for four generations. She didn't even glance back at the rambling lodge, the weathered barn or the outbuildings. Nor take a last-minute look at the dry riverbed that once became an angry torrent that threatened to inundate the ranch. But that was many years ago, before the river was dammed and the reservoir built. She averted her eyes from her herb garden and her son's tree house. Instead she forced herself to keep her eyes on the two-lane road bordered on both sides by the fallow fields of Bar B Ranch land.

''Imagine if we were Pony Express riders,'' she said with determined cheerfulness to the boy next to her who was hunched down in his seat, his baseball cap pulled low over his eyes. ''Galloping across the country, carrying the mail to Diamond Springs, Dry Wells and Reese River and finally..."

"We're not," Dylan said glumly.

"Yes, but what if we were?" she continued, resolutely putting the best face on things by pointing out how much worse off they could be. "Our horses would be getting tired and there'd be robbers and hostile Indians after us. And if it was raining..."

"It doesn't rain here," he said.

"Not very often. But sometimes it does. Sometimes we've even had flash floods in the past, according to Grandpa. But we don't care. We keep our horses going right through the water and wind and rain, because our job is to deliver the mail, and the mail must go through," she said brightly.

She reached for him, to pat his shoulder, or tug affectionately at his cap, but he shifted away from her, and his rejection was like an arrow piercing her heart. Her son leaned against the door and turned his head away. But not before she saw a tear slide down his sun-tanned cheek. Her heart turned over and she swallowed over a lump in her throat. She couldn't cry in front of him. She couldn't cry at all. He mustn't know how much it hurt her to take him away from the only home he'd ever known. Crying was a sign of weakness and she had to be strong. For her son and for herself.

"Look, Dylan, it's not going to be so bad. In some ways it's going to be better, living in town. It's close to work, so I can come home for lunch. Check up on you. And it's closer to your school, and it's..."

"School's out. It's summer," he muttered, his face pressed against the window.

"I know that. But what about your friends,

and…and…'' Even she, the original Pollyanna, was running out of advantages of living in Silverado, population 670, one of Nevada's oldest mining towns, as opposed to the Silver Springs Ranch—the place where she'd carved her initials in an old oak tree like generations of McIntyres before her, where her father had taught her to ride a horse when she could barely walk, and her mother had taught her to quilt and put up preserves for the winter. All the things she thought she and Dylan's father would teach him. Who would have thought it would end like this—her and her son in a rattletrap truck packed high with their most precious possessions, their backs to the land they loved?

In the distant heat, waves rose from the blacktop and the sun glittered on a distant field making it shimmer like a lake. But this was high desert, and the image of a lake was only a mirage. Was her hope of a bright future for her and her son a mirage, as well? She had to make it work. She had to.

''When my daddy comes back we're gonna move back home, aren't we?'' he said.

Laura gripped the steering wheel so tightly, her fingers hurt. Dylan had gone almost an hour today without mentioning his father. Which was some kind of record. It was better than yesterday and the day before. But not good enough. She'd finally told him the truth. As painful as it was. He had to hear it from her before he heard it from someone else. That his daddy wasn't coming back. But he didn't believe her. Wouldn't believe her. Even though she'd signed the final divorce papers and had them in her purse at that very moment.

''When my daddy comes back,'' Dylan continued,

''he's gonna bring me a remote-controlled airplane and a new saddle and a ten-speed bike. When he comes down the road in his new sports car, I'm gonna be waiting in my tree house.''

''Dylan...'' she cautioned. ''It's not your tree house anymore. It's not our ranch. It's not our home.'' The effort it took to say the words made her throat hurt.

''How's my dad gonna find me if I'm not in my tree house?'' he demanded. ''We gotta go back. We can't sell the ranch.''

''We have sold the ranch,'' she explained patiently for the hundredth time. ''But Silverado is a small town. All he'd have to do is ask where we are. He could find you. But...'' *But he doesn't want to find you. Doesn't care enough about you or me...*

''He *is* coming.'' Dylan glared at her, his hands clenched into small fists. ''Don't you say he isn't.''

She pressed her lips together. She wouldn't say it. Not again. Because she couldn't bear to repeat the words that would break his heart. *Your daddy isn't coming back.*

THE HOUSE WAS EXACTLY the way it looked in the pictures. Adirondack-style, built of natural pine logs, hauled from a faraway forest over one hundred years ago and nestled in a valley with a view of the surrounding bare mountains from every room. When he arrived an hour ago, Brandon Marsh had set his suitcases and his notebook computer in the middle of the living room and gone to look around, satisfied with the simple but comfortable chairs covered in geometric design, the matching couch along the wall and the braid rug. He'd insisted the furnishings come with the house, and the owner had agreed. As well she should, at the price he'd paid.

He wanted nothing of his past life in this house—not a picture, not a stick of furniture. Nothing to remind him of what he'd lost. The best part was the acres of land separating him from the rest of the world. Except for an occasional trip to town for supplies, he didn't need to see anyone. Like the woman and child and man who used to live in this house, whose photo he'd found forgotten on the mantel. At least he assumed that's who they were.

In any case he quickly turned the picture facedown and would pack it up along with a book on herbs from the kitchen counter and mail it to their forwarding address. That way he'd never have to meet them. Never have to see them in person. The picture was bad enough. A woman with a mass of dark curly hair, her arm around a boy with two front teeth missing and a man standing behind them staring at the camera. The sight of them caused a pain in his chest. A pain where his heart used to be before the accident. He had a picture like that. Three people bound together by love and by blood. That picture which had also once graced a mantel, was now at the bottom of a cardboard box he had no intention of unpacking. Not for a long, long time.

He'd timed his arrival just right. Because although he was anxious to move in, he certainly didn't want to run into the former owners and be forced to engage in small talk. In fact, he'd driven by the ranch once to make sure there was no vehicle in the driveway before he drove in. He didn't want to hear any stories they had to tell about the good times spent in that house, where they put their Christmas tree, how they raised their cows and horses and about the generations who'd grown up there, and so on and so on.

But he hadn't missed the McIntyres by much, not if the warm ashes in the massive stone fireplace were any indication. And the lingering aroma of fresh bread baking that emanated from the kitchen. He threw open the front door and then shoved the windows open to air the place out. No warm hearths for him. No homey scents. Just the wide-open spaces, thank you, and peace and quiet, and most important—solitude.

Just then the peace and quiet were shattered by the clatter of a poorly tuned truck with a bad muffler. Before he could shut the front door and hang out a Do Not Disturb sign, a small boy in faded jeans walked in the front door and tiptoed up the stairs without noticing the new owner.

''Hold it,'' Brandon said. ''Where do you think you're going?''

''Forgot my Legos,'' the boy said, his head whipping around at the sound of a strange voice. Still, the kid was cool. He scarcely missed a beat. As if he wasn't at all surprised to find a strange man in his house. He looked down from the landing from under a Colorado Rockies baseball cap and surveyed Brandon with almost casual curiosity.

Brandon ran his hand through his hair. It was the kid in the picture. Who'd forgotten his Legos. Damn, damn, damn. How could Brandon have missed the Legos? Because he hadn't gone into the boy's room. He didn't want to see a stray baseball trading card or a small action figure or a wall with pictures of football players on it or any evidence of the boy who used to live there. But now he was face-to-face with the boy himself. Complete with freckles and missing teeth. He clenched his jaw and steeled himself for a brief exchange. The briefer the better.

But the boy was in no hurry. "Who're you?" he asked, resting his chin on the banister and peering down at him.

"I'm the new owner of the house," he said. The boy's mouth turned down at the corners and he scowled. Maybe he shouldn't have said it so bluntly, Brandon thought. Maybe the kid didn't want to face the fact that there was a new owner. Probably not. But that wasn't his problem. He just wished the kid wouldn't look at him like that. Both mad and sad at the same time. As if he'd stolen his house from him. When he'd actually bought it at a fair price from the woman who, according to the real estate agent, was "extremely motivated to sell."

"You got any kids?" the boy asked.

"No." He didn't mean to spit out the word so harshly, but he didn't want to be reminded of his loss. As if he could ever forget.

The boy was undaunted. The questioning continued. "What do you want to live in a big house for if you got no kids?" he asked, scratching his ear.

Brandon took a deep breath. This was just the kind of conversation he didn't want to have. With anyone. But especially not with a little boy who used to live here. "I like the house," he said. Then he glanced out the front window at the spectacular view of the vast valley ringed with jagged mountains, the most beautiful valley in the West, according to the Realtor. But the view meant nothing to Brandon, only what it stood for—isolation. Isolation from pitying looks, well-meaning friends and memories. Memories too painful to bear. "And I like the land."

"I like my tree house," the boy said.

"Tree house? You have a tree house? Aren't you taking it with you?" Brandon certainly didn't want a tree house on his property.

"Can't. We're movin' to town." The boy frowned and pulled his cap down over his forehead. "But when my daddy comes back we're movin' back."

"I see," Brandon said. There was no point in arguing with an eight-year-old or thereabouts. But he wondered if the boy's mother encouraged these fantasies or even knew about them. He thought he'd understood from the Realtor that the parents were divorced and that her dwindling finances were the cause of the sale of the property.

Speaking of which, he could hear the sound of a truck's engine idling in the driveway. If that was the boy's mother waiting for him, how long would it be before she came in to see what was taking so long? He had no desire to meet her, now or later.

"I'll come up with you," Brandon said. "See what else you forgot."

The boy shrugged and led the way down the hall to his room. It was worse than he'd thought. There were bunk beds, stripped of sheets and blankets, the kind of beds he'd imagined buying for his own son when he'd outgrown his crib. A bookshelf meant for books to be read at night before bed, as he'd planned to read to his son. And there were Legos, too, but they were just a blur as Brandon turned around swiftly, unable to take in another detail of the boy's room without losing it completely.

He had to get out of there. Fortunately the kid

didn't notice. Didn't notice that Brandon had bolted, gone downstairs and out onto the veranda to take a breath of air. From there he could see the woman waiting in the truck with the engine running, her forehead resting against the steering wheel, her dark hair tumbled over her shoulders. The whole image was such a picture of dejection he was jerked out of his own despair for just a moment. It occurred to him she might have problems beyond just leaving her home.

All the more reason to avoid her. But for some reason he found himself stepping off the porch and walking up to her side window. He felt compelled to say something reassuring, but he knew firsthand how empty words can be when your world falls apart. Besides, what did he know about her problems? Instead, what he should do was to speak to her about not coming back to retrieve lost objects whenever she felt like it. She had to understand it was his house now and that visitors were not welcome. Especially the kind of visitor who reminded him of the family he once had.

She must've heard his shoes crunch on the gravel, because she sat up, her spine rigid against the bucket seat. She turned and surveyed him through huge, sad hazel eyes. She tried to smile, but her lips trembled, and he felt a pang of sympathy for her.

Sympathy—what good did that do anybody? With an effort he hardened his heart. So she was sad to leave her homestead. There were worse things in this world. She should have figured out a way to save it. Was it his fault that he needed a house in the country and she needed the money?

"I'm sorry about intruding on you like this," she

said in a tremulous voice. ''But my son forgot his—''

''His Legos, I know. I hope it won't happen again.''

She paled under the smattering of freckles on her cheekbones. Maybe people in small towns in Nevada didn't talk that way to their neighbors. But he'd moved to a ranch so he wouldn't have any neighbors. If he'd wanted neighbors he could have stayed in San Francisco. He wouldn't have people dropping in on him like this.

''It won't. I mean, it can't,'' the woman said. ''He only has one set of Legos and he left them under his bed. If we hadn't been in such a hurry to get out before you got here…''

''I appreciate your closing on the house sale and moving out so promptly, but…''

''But you want us to leave. I understand.'' The woman leaned on her horn. The harsh noise shattered the quiet country air, but it had the desired effect. The boy came running out of the house with a large plastic box under his arm and jumped in the truck.

She glanced at Brandon and took a deep breath. ''Look, Mr.—Mr. Marsh, isn't it? I'm really sorry about this. I realize you're looking for privacy and I assure you you've come to the right place. If there's anything I can do to help you get settled, show you around town or introduce you to some people, whatever—''

''That won't be necessary,'' he said. ''Goodbye.''

''Goodbye, mister,'' the boy said with a wave of his hand. ''Be seeing you.''

No, you won't, Brandon thought. *Not if I can help it.* But he waved anyway. It was just an automatic gesture. It wasn't because he couldn't stand to see any more disappointment on the small face pressed against the side window.

The woman didn't give him a backward glance. Her balding tires squealed on the gravel before she shifted again and tore down the driveway as if she was just as anxious as he was to put an end to their meeting.

"Get those valves adjusted," he yelled. She probably didn't hear him. And if she did, she probably wouldn't do it. She looked like the stubborn type. With her freckles and determined chin. What did it matter to him if she let the truck fall apart? If it died on that deserted road out there? Where they'd be stuck on that empty road with their household goods. Maybe she intended to junk the truck and buy a new car when they got to town. Now that she had his money she could certainly afford it. That and a house in town. At least that's what the Realtor Byron "Buzz" Busby had said when Brandon asked why the owner was selling the most beautiful piece of land in Nevada.

"Financial difficulties as well as a desire to move to town. The way Laura tells it, she's had enough of livin' so far out. Be closer to her aunt, too, who's ailing. There're folks who'll tell you the real reason has more to do with that no-good, rotten, no-account bastard and the way he ran through her money...but here I go, tellin' tales out of school," Mr. Busby had said. "Suffice it to say that I could've sold that ranch a hundred times over. It's a city dweller's dream with good airport access, a plentiful water supply thanks to your own reservoir and views to die for. Yep, you got it 'cause you outbid everybody else, Mr. Marsh. I'm sure you're gonna be happy there."

Happy? He didn't count on being happy there or anywhere. He'd be satisfied not to feel anything. No pain, no joy, no happiness. Nothing. That was his goal. To become numb. To get through just one night without his recurring nightmares. And then one more. One step at a time. To wake up in the morning without a black cloud hanging over his head. That's why he was there. If it didn't work, he'd… He didn't know what he'd do. He'd tried everything else. And he'd reached the end of his rope.

LAURA HAD the distinct feeling that everyone in town stopped what they were doing to turn to watch her drive through town on her way toward her aunt Emily's remodeled Victorian. She could almost hear the whispers behind the shutters. The talk behind closed doors.

"Oh, how the mighty are fallen."

"Serves her right for marrying an outsider."

"Heard she made a bundle on the ranch. Been McIntyres there since anyone can remember."

"Sold out to a city slicker who paid through the nose for the privilege of living like a McIntyre."

"Gonna turn it into a shopping center, I heard."

"Or a dude ranch."

"Good thing her daddy didn't live to see it, or her granddaddy, the mayor."

"Or her great-granddaddy, the prospector."

She chastised herself for her overly active imagination. Told herself there were no voices. No one cared what had happened to her. But still she stared straight ahead, afraid to catch anyone's eye, afraid of what she might see there—pity, compassion, embarrassment, condolences. Whatever it was, she didn't want it. She knew they weren't bad people, just curious.

It wasn't a bad town, as towns went. Like so many of Nevada's boom-and-bust small towns, it was founded when gold and silver were discovered there one hundred and twenty-five years ago and had been in a state of genteel decline ever since the mines played out.

Left behind were a handful of hardy souls and the hollow monuments to the past. The old opera house, the hotel, the brothel and the Front Street row of stately Victorian houses with their gingerbread trim. All saved from destruction by the Silverado Historical Society, founded by her father.

And on Main Street—the nuts and bolts of the present-day community—the drugstore, the hardware store, the café and the feed-and-fuel. No, it wasn't a bad town, it was just that she'd never imagined living there. She was born on the ranch, was brought up there and always assumed she'd live her whole life there like her parents and grandparents before her. But that was before she met Jason Bradley. And made the biggest mistake of her life.

''Why do we hafta stay with Aunt Em?'' Dylan asked as they pulled into the circular driveway of her aunt's bed-and-breakfast.

''Because she invited us. She's family. About all I've got left of my family. And she has room for us. And we'll be able to help her out while she's recovering from her surgery. But it's just temporary. Until Willa Mae Miner leaves and I get my promotion. Then we get to live in her apartment over the post office. There's a park across the street. You'll like that.''

''No, I won't. I don't like parks. I'm not a baby. I wanna go home. I wanna go home now and wait for my daddy to come back,'' he wailed.

Laura sighed and looked at her son for a long moment. At his shaggy, sunbleached hair, his stubborn chin and at the holes in the knees of his jeans. And remembered when he was a baby. A round-faced, chubby-cheeked angel. Her baby. But he was right, he wasn't a baby anymore. This would be so much easier if he was. Then there wouldn't be these painfully tiring explanations. She was tired—tired of being a single parent, tired of covering up, tired of being brave, of keeping a stiff upper lip when all she wanted to do was join in and cry along with him, ''I wanna go home.''

''I don't like Aunt Emily,'' he said crossly as they parked in the driveway next to a new Dodge sport utility vehicle and her aunt's station wagon. So they weren't the only guests tonight.

''Of course you like her. You just don't know her very well. This is a chance for us both to get reacquainted with her. Aunt Emily is being very kind to let us stay here, and don't you forget it,'' she said sternly. ''Besides, she's a wonderful cook.'' Emily Eckhart watched every cooking show available on cable TV and was the founder of the Silverado gourmet club. When she turned her empty nest into a bed-and-breakfast, she offered dinners, too, for a price her guests seemed willing to pay. As she said with a twinkle in her eye, ''It keeps me out of trouble.''

Dylan curled his lip. ''She makes yucky food.''

''I'll have you know people drive for miles to stay

here and eat her 'yucky' food,'' Laura said. To Dylan, ''yucky'' meant rich sauces, undercooked vegetables and her specialty—poached salmon with hollandaise sauce. Laura would never admit it, but there was one drawback to staying at her aunt's which had nothing to do with the ''yucky'' food. That was the fact that Emily might gently pry into her niece's affairs, and when she found out anything, it would soon be all over town. Laura wanted to be forthcoming with her mother's sister, and yet she was worried about being an object of pity.

''And she's got yucky stuff in her house,'' he added.

''That 'yucky stuff' is the antiques she's spent a lifetime collecting, young man. So don't knock anything over.''

Laura appreciated Emily's food and her artifacts—treasures such as the spinning wheel in the living room and the butter churn in the one of the bedrooms. Her mother, too, had collected antiques. What a shame Laura had had to sell most of them in the past year. How many times her aunt and her mother had taken little Laura along on their forays in the countryside, to a garage sale here or an auction there. She'd watch as they bargained, then she'd ride home in the back seat of the car, nestled between an end table and an old oak chair they planned to refinish or a silk-tasseled ottoman to be reupholstered.

How could she blame Aunt Emily for being a gossip? Who wasn't, when gossip was one of the main pleasures of life in Silverado, along with bingo on Thursday nights in the church basement. Aunt Emily was family. Family Laura desperately needed at a time like this. Like the antiques and the land she'd been selling off for the past year, the family members had dwindled down to a precious few.

''Hellooo,'' her aunt called from the front steps, wiping her hands on a frilly apron.

Laura grabbed her suitcase, nudged her son until he reluctantly slid out of his seat and even more reluctantly climbed the front steps and kissed his great-aunt on the cheek. She only hoped Aunt Em didn't see him rub the kiss off with the back of his hand immediately afterward.

''How are you feeling?'' Laura asked, noting that her usually robust aunt looked as if she'd shed a few pounds since her surgery.

''Just fine, dear. If you wouldn't mind pulling your truck around to the rear and coming in through the back door,'' her aunt suggested, ''that would be lovely.''

''Oh, of course.'' She should have thought of it herself. How incongruous an old truck partially covered with a blue plastic tarpaulin looked in front of an impeccably restored Victorian house. Incongruous was putting it mildly. It looked awful. She and Dylan didn't look so good, either, in their jeans and T-shirts, which was probably why Emily had suggested they go in the back door. After all, they weren't guests, they were poor relations.

Before they went inside via the back entrance, Dylan demanded that Laura get his bicycle out of the back of the truck. She had no idea where it was in the pile of household goods under the tarp and she was too tired to go looking for it. And too depressed.

''Tomorrow,'' she said wearily. ''We'll find it tomorrow.''

"I want it now," he said, hopping up onto the fender.

She gave in as usual. Unable to resist his determination, wanting to make up for moving him away from the only home he'd ever known, for the lack of a father in his life, wanting to see him smile, wanting so much...for so long.

It took at least fifteen minutes of routing through their belongings, but when they uncovered his bike, his shout of glee made Laura almost forget her fatigue. Her aunt waved off her offer to help with dinner, and when Laura walked into the dining room she felt like a guest instead of a poor relation.

AUNT EMILY PRESIDED over the large oval dinner table with all the dignity of the wife of the gold baron who'd lived there one hundred years ago. The two other guests at the town's only B and B were from Los Angeles, taking a tour of historic silver mining towns, taking a turn at panning for gold, visiting the museum and shopping for silver jewelry. They knew nothing about Laura or her circumstances. Not yet, anyway. Not that they weren't curious.

"You mean you were born and raised right here in Silverado?" the silver-haired retired schoolteacher asked Laura over apple dumplings.

"About five miles outside of town," she said.

"We live on a ranch," Dylan said, licking his spoon for the last remnant of caramel cinnamon sauce.

"With horses and cows?" the woman asked.

"We had to sell the stock on account of—" Dylan began.

"Our moving to town," Laura interrupted. Heaven

only knew what Dylan was going to say. Or what he really knew about his father's disappearance.

"Some day when my daddy comes back we're gonna get it all back," he said. "The cows and the horses and a new car. Aren't we, Mom?"

"We'll see," Laura said with a forced smile. Inside she was cringing. She knew she should deny that her ex-husband was coming back, but this was not a good time. Not in front of strangers, her aunt and Dylan.

"How nice," the woman said. "Where is your daddy now?"

"He's on a business trip," her son said importantly. That had been the official story of why Jason was never around. One that sounded better than saying he'd deserted his wife and child when he'd used up their resources on his get-rich-quick schemes.

"What kind of business does he do?" the other woman asked.

Laura paused to wonder how a stranger, a woman she'd never seen before tonight, had the nerve to pepper her son with questions. She stifled the urge to tell the woman to mind her own business. But the woman was her aunt's guest, and a paying one at that. And she was being altogether too sensitive. People were going to wonder, people were going to ask. She'd better get used to it.

"He's in sales," her aunt interjected sparing Laura the humiliation of admitting her ex-husband's only job for the past nine years was spending her money on one scheme after another. She shot her aunt a grateful look, then changed the subject by directing a question at the woman. "How do you like Silverado?"

"It's a charming little town."

"It sucks," Dylan said.

Laura frowned at her son and nudged him under the table. "You may be excused," she said.

He slid off his seat and was out the back door in a flash. The guests looked at each other, her aunt changed the subject and the guests finally left for a walk down Main Street, which was slowly being upgraded with gas lamps by the historical society.

"I apologize for Dylan, Aunt Emily. He's going through a bad time right now. Leaving the ranch has been hard on him."

"Of course it has. Poor little fatherless boy. You don't really expect Jason back at all, do you?" her aunt asked, her eyes brimming with sympathy.

Laura sighed. She took a deep breath, prepared to launch into the familiar lies she'd been telling since he left town. Then she stopped and shook her head. "No," she said softly. "I don't."

Her aunt placed one bejeweled hand on Laura's arm. "There, that wasn't so hard to say, was it? You know, it's not your fault what happened. And most everyone knows a divorce was in the works. So why not just come out with it?"

Laura shook her head. "I will. It's just… It's not easy. It's one thing to know deep inside it's over. It's another to say the words out loud. I'm divorced."

"Come, dear. You did everything you could to hold things together. I know it and I suspect most other folks know it, too."

"Dylan doesn't," Laura said, her voice quavering slightly. "All he knows is that his father is gone. You wouldn't think a father could turn his back on his son and never see him again, would you? But that's exactly what has happened. Jason has a new life a thousand miles from here. Our divorce is final now and he's out of the picture. I've told Dylan that. But he doesn't want to accept it."

"He's only eight," her aunt said gently. "It will take him some time to get used to the idea."

"I know. I know." Laura sighed. "I expect too much of him, I guess."

Her aunt nodded, and the unmistakable sympathy on her face was a reminder of why Laura hadn't told her before. She'd rather have anything than pity. She'd prefer stupefaction, incredulity or disdain. But she no longer had the luxury of hiding behind half-truths and downright lies. She'd told her aunt, and soon the whole town would know. They'd know that Jason wasn't coming back, but they didn't have to know how he'd run through her money. They didn't have to know how naive she'd been, how trusting. Or how ambitious he was, how frustrated with his own failures and with her lack of understanding. And how he'd finally taken off to seek his fortune elsewhere.

She knew it was for the best. She only wished he hadn't deserted his son as well as his wife. But it was over now and she was on her own. Older, poorer and a little wiser, she hoped. She'd had to pay dearly for that wisdom, and she'd be paying for a long, long time, too. She'd never be able to quit her job; she needed a steady income. Thank heavens she had a job.

"That was a wonderful dinner, Aunt Em," she said, changing the subject. "How are you feeling?"

"Much better. Not quite up to par yet. But coming along. The doctor says another six weeks."

"You should take it easy."

"I know, but I have a business to run. I'm hoping to be booked up for the whole season."

"Oh, dear. I'm afraid we're imposing. If we weren't here..."

"If you weren't here I wouldn't have this chance for a good visit with you. Ever since your husband left, you've been strangers. Rushing right home after work, burying yourself in the country. I've missed you."

"I've missed you, too." It was true. It was good to have someone to talk to. Someone who'd known her all her life. Someone who loved her. She hadn't felt like socializing in a long time. Hadn't invited even her aunt out to the ranch. Let holidays slide by with excuses she was too busy. She was busy—busy making excuses for her husband's absence. Covering up. "Maybe I can help out with the cooking and cleaning while I'm here," she suggested.

"Don't even think about it. I have two local girls who come by every day to do the laundry and clean. No offense, but I don't trust the cooking to anyone but myself. You may not know this, but the bed-and-breakfast was just my excuse to cook for people. I've always wanted to have a restaurant of my own. But the failure rate of new restaurants is phenomenal. Whereas B and B's seem to do well. At least around here I have no competition. So when I expanded into dinners I thought I'd open them up to townspeople, but evidently they prefer the coffee shop. Most of them, anyway. So what can you do?" She paused. "By the way, does he know you've sold the ranch?" her aunt asked.

"Jason? No, he doesn't. And yet he couldn't be

that surprised.'' She crumpled her napkin in her hand. She hated talking about her ex-husband. It was painful to admit she'd made such a big mistake in marrying someone she barely knew. Her only consolation was that she had Dylan. The light of her life. Without him she'd have nothing left.

''I've learned one thing, Auntie. I'm not cut out for marriage. I don't have what it takes—the patience, the understanding, the...the stick-to-itiveness... I don't have it.''

''Come now, dear. You're being too hard on yourself. Everyone gets another chance at marriage. Especially you and maybe even me.'' Emily winked at her niece.

Laura's mouth fell open in surprise. What did her aunt mean when she said ''even me''? Aunt Emily had been widowed for many years and her son Andrew lived across the country. If she wanted to remarry, more power to her. But she'd had, by all accounts, a happy marriage. Evidently it was all the more reason to want to repeat the experience. Whereas Laura had only negative thoughts about marriage. Maybe someday they'd fade. But by the time they did, she'd be rocking on her front porch, telling her grandchildren stories about the history of Silverado. Maybe they'd be more interested in the old days than Dylan was.

Laura gave her aunt a curious look. ''Do you have anyone special in mind?''

''For you or for me?'' her aunt asked, her eyes wide, but a faint tinge of pink on her cheeks.

''Well, I thought...''

''We're talking about you, dear. You're much too young to give up on men at your age.''

Laura shook her head. ‘‘I don’t feel young. I feel as old as those hills out there. One marriage was enough for me. More than enough.’’ Laura stood, but her aunt put her hand on her arm and poured her a second cup of coffee from a silver urn.

‘‘Sit down. Relax. You’ve had a hard day,’’ her aunt insisted, and she couldn’t deny it. It had been one of the hardest days of her life. But relax? She couldn’t relax until her debts were paid off.

‘‘Thanks again for letting us stay here. Now, if you won’t let me help out, I want to pay you, of course.’’

‘‘No relation of mine will pay to stay with me. Why, if your dear mother were here…’’

Thank God she wasn’t. She’d told Laura not to marry Jason. She’d never have said, ‘‘I told you so,’’ but she would have thought it. And it would have broken her heart to see the ranch sold.

After a momentary pause to wipe her eyes with an embroidered handkerchief, her aunt continued. ‘‘Now, tell me more about the new owner.’’

‘‘Well…’’ Talking about the new owner was certainly preferable to talking about her ex-husband. But not by much. ‘‘I don’t know anything about him. Only that he appears to be living there alone. And he drives a fancy black sports car. I saw it in the driveway. I know he doesn’t like kids.’’

‘‘What does he look like?’’ her aunt asked.

‘‘Like he’s made of granite.’’

‘‘Granite?’’ he aunt asked, looking perplexed. ‘‘You mean like Mount Rushmore?’’

‘‘Yes, only colder and more distant,’’ Laura said.

‘‘That’s not what I heard from Alice Gray, whose sister saw him at the discount store on the highway.

She said he looked like that movie star...what's his name?''

''Darth Maul?'' Laura teased, naming one of Dylan's toy action figures.

Her aunt pursed her lips together. ''I haven't seen him, but I don't think so. Seriously, and looks aside, if he has a fancy sports car and he paid cash for your ranch, I'd say he must have something going for him.''

''Yes,'' Laura said. ''He must have money. But money isn't everything.'' She couldn't help feeling bitter. Money wasn't everything, but if you didn't have it, it sure seemed like it was everything.

''How old would you say he was?'' her aunt asked, deliberately overlooking the bitter tone in her niece's voice.

''I don't know... In his thirties, I guess. I could be wrong. I could be wrong about his looks, too. Maybe he looks like Tom Cruise and I didn't notice. I only saw him briefly. Outside the house this morning.'' Just long enough to notice steel-gray eyes and a cynical mouth that never smiled. She gave a little shiver just remembering.

''Seems a shame, a single city man rattling around in that big five-bedroom house in the middle of that thousand-acre ranch, doesn't it?'' Emily asked, propping her plump elbows on the white tablecloth and gazing at her niece.

''I suppose so.'' A shame? It was a crime. It was a house meant for a family. A big family. At one time she'd imagined kids in every one of the five bedrooms. The one with the bunk beds was Dylan's. The one at the end of the hall with the flowered wallpaper had been hers when she was a child. Which one would the tall stranger sleep in? What did it matter? It was his now. His to change, alter, remodel...and she'd better get used to it.

"I don't understand it, but maybe he's not single and his family will be joining him later," her aunt suggested.

"I have no idea. I swear, Aunt Em, I've only spoken ten words to the man, if that. Buzz probably told me something about him when we closed the sale, but I wasn't paying attention. If anyone can find out the details, it will be you."

Her aunt nodded solemnly. "I intend to," she said.

THERE WAS AT LEAST ONE benefit to living in town, Laura reminded herself as she walked briskly down Main Street to work the next morning. She didn't have to worry that her truck would break down on the way to work. Or that Dylan would fall out of his tree house and break his leg while she was at work. She walked briskly, but she should have been running. She was late as usual. And today she had no excuse. She was living only a few blocks away.

But today, as was usual these days, she got bogged down in a no-win argument with her son over the new rules.

"Don't ride your bike any farther than the cemetery."

"Check with me before you go anywhere."

"Be home for lunch at twelve."

Every rule was cause for an objection on his part followed by an argument. She suggested for the umpteenth time that he go to the day camp the church was running, but he said it was for babies. So she dropped the subject.

She wished she'd had time for breakfast. The smell of Aunt Em's blueberry muffins wafting from the kitchen had caused her mouth to water and her stomach to growl. In the old days, not that long ago, she'd have coffee at her breakfast nook, look out toward the valley at Silver Springs ranch land stretching as far as the eye could see, listen to the red-wing orioles and watch the cattle graze. The wells would be pumping water to irrigate the fertile fields. The cattle were gone now, sold months ago to pay for the roof repair, along with the horses, the tractor and the flatbed truck. All that was left was Dylan's tree house and her herb garden.

The phone was ringing inside the post office and there were three people standing outside, waiting to get in. One was Wes Blandings, the retired plumber. He was always there. No matter how early she got there, he was waiting outside.

"You're late again, Laura. Run into a lot of traffic, did you?" he asked sarcastically. They both knew there was no traffic on her road. But the poor man had nothing to do but wait impatiently for the mail. Even though it didn't come in until two in the afternoon, he checked his box first thing in the morning.

"No traffic today, Wes," she said as pleasantly as she could while she unlocked the door. It wouldn't do to tell him his box was empty and was likely to remain so until his retirement check came. The postmistress in a small town knew everything about the inhabitants. Too much. She had to dispense hope as well as the mail. Not that she was the postmistress. Not yet.

"I've moved to town, Wes. No more commuting." Might as well come out with it. Wes would find out soon enough. Along with the rest of the town.

''That right? Heard you sold your place,'' he said, following her into the tiny building. ''Heard the new owner needed a place to hide out from the law.''

''Really?'' Laura said.

Georgianna Breck, who was standing behind him, chimed in. ''That's not what I heard. I heard he's going to turn it into a theme park.''

Laura almost choked. ''A theme park? I don't think so.'' She slipped behind the counter and grabbed the phone.

''Silverado Post Office. Acting Assistant Postmistress speaking,'' she said.

''This is Brandon Marsh at the Silver Springs Ranch. What time is the mail delivery?''

Chapter Two

Laura froze. She could see him now, sitting in *her* kitchen, looking out *her* window at *her* view. Expecting to have his mail neatly delivered to his doorstep. Where did he think he was? San Francisco? She took a deep breath.

"There is no mail delivery on your road. Your mail is here in the post office, if you have any."

"In the post office? I don't believe this. Why didn't someone tell me?"

"I—I'm sorry. It's my fault. I should have informed you. I might be able to find someone who was going out your way to drop it off, but..."

"No, that won't be necessary. I'll come in to pick it up. How can it be possible in this day and age that you don't have a delivery service? I'm going to file a complaint with the post office in... Where does your mail come from?"

"You do that," she said, knowing it would do no good. The post office would never send someone to deliver mail to a spread-out, rural community like theirs. "It comes from Reno." She scanned the line of people that now snaked out the front door. "Now, if you'll excuse me..."

"Wait a minute. What time does the mail come in?"

"Two o'clock." She hung up.

Laura forced herself to concentrate on the customers. But she couldn't stop thinking of the man who'd bought her house. Should she have told him about the lack of mail service? Should she have told him he could complain all he wanted, but he didn't have a hope in hell of having his mail delivered? He now lived in a rural area and that was one of the disadvantages. She'd never seen it as such, but for someone used to city life…

Absently she rewrapped a poorly taped package for Dora Hayslip. Then she had to leaf through big books to find the commemorative stamps the next customer wanted. When she finally finished with the customers, she had to sort mail that had come in on Saturday. She saw several letters for Brandon Marsh, and it gave her a jolt to see someone else's name above the name of her ranch. No, *his* ranch. She was as bad as her son. Having a hard time letting go. She wondered if he'd come in today. She found herself watching the clock.

At lunchtime, Cecily, the part-time girl came in, and Laura hurried back to Aunt Em's. To her relief Dylan was actually sitting on the front steps of the house waiting for her. His jeans were ripped, his face was dirty and he had a cut on his finger.

"What happened to you?" she asked.

"Nothing."

"Where have you been?"

"No place," he said. "Aunt Emily's in bed."

"What?"

"I went in there and I seen her in her room. Isn't she kinda old for a nap?"

Laura ordered him to clean up, then rushed down the hall to see her aunt.

"Just resting," her aunt said when Laura asked her what she was doing. "I didn't sleep well last night." She looked pale, and there were dark circles under her eyes that hadn't been there last night.

"Shall I call the doctor?" Laura asked.

"No need. He told me there'd be days like this and he told me what to do. I've taken my medicine and I'm resting."

"What about your guests?" Laura asked anxiously.

"They left this morning. The girls changed the sheets and we're all set for the next group tonight."

"Are you sure you shouldn't cancel?"

"Oh, no. But I may cancel dinner. I hate to do it, but I could send them to the diner." Her aunt's mouth turned down at the corners at the thought of her guests eating at such an inferior place.

"Let me cook the dinner for you," Laura said. "That is, if you trust me."

"Of course I trust you," her aunt said without much conviction in her voice. "But I couldn't ask you—"

"Really, I'd love to."

"Well...if you're sure."

"I'm sure. Now you rest," she said. "And I'll try to leave work early tonight."

She made sandwiches for her and Dylan and took one up to her aunt with a cup of tea before she left. When she walked out the front door, Dylan was sitting on the steps where she'd found him an hour ago, his arms folded around his knees with a morose frown on his face. She stood there for a long moment without speaking, not knowing what to say to him.

"I don't like it here. I wanna go home," he said.

We don't have a home were the only words that came to her mind. She didn't say them. Couldn't say them. Instead, she turned around, kneeled down on the steps and hugged him tightly. "I know you do. But right now we have to stay here. Just for a while. Just until we get settled in our new home."

"I don't want a new home."

His words hurt like the hot brand of the familiar SS of the Silver Springs Ranch. She didn't want a new home, either. She wanted her old home with its warmth and security and memories wrapped around her like a blanket. The pain of leaving it, of feeling guilty for losing it, was like a knife in her heart. Every time Dylan complained about leaving or waiting for his father, he twisted the knife.

"I miss my tree house," he said.

"We'll build a new one," she said, unwrapping her arms and gazing at him, willing him to be patient, to be happy. "Just as soon as we get settled."

He shook his head. "Don't want a new one."

"It'll be bigger and better than your old house. I'll stop by the hardware store and see how much the boards cost."

"We got boards at the ranch."

"Yes, but..." She bit her tongue. She'd sold the place "as is," lock, stock and barrel. Boards included. She couldn't tell Dylan that. It would just start another argument that nobody would win.

"Are we poor?" he asked, regarding her with a worried frown.

"Of course we're not poor," she said brightly. "But we don't waste money, either. We've got money for the things we need. And a new tree house is one of them. As soon as I get my new job and we get our own place, everything will be okay. Can you hold on until then?" she asked, taking his hands in hers and squeezing tightly.

He didn't answer. She couldn't expect him to understand. His whole world had been turned upside down. She sighed and hugged him again.

"I have to go back to work now. You know where to find me if you need me."

He nodded, but he looked so forlorn, she felt sick about leaving him there. But she was already late. Cecily would be chomping at the bit, anxious to get back to her other job at the coffee shop, and Laura couldn't afford a single black mark against her if she was to be named postmistress. She took a few steps, then turned to look back. Dylan was still sitting there, his head resting on his knees, looking as if he'd lost his best friend. But this was worse. He'd lost his father, his home and his tree house.

Brandon Marsh came into the post office at precisely two o'clock. The place was full of customers. The driver of the mail truck had dumped the bags in back and she hadn't had a moment to sort through them. She'd told him the mail was in at two and now he was here, but the mail wasn't ready. A hush fell over the small office as all heads swerved in his direction. She couldn't blame them. So little happened in Silverado. A newcomer was fair game. Someone to stare at, speculate about, discuss and dissect.

Laura was just as bad as everyone else. She wanted to stare at him too. To see if he looked as forbidding as he did the last time she'd seen him. But she only allowed herself a brief glance before she trained her eyes on Amanda Little, the librarian who was mailing a package to her niece in Las Vegas.

"What do you think, Laura? Should I insure it or not? It's only cookies, but you know how Mimi's counting on them. I made chocolate chip this time."

"How much did you say it was worth?" Her voice sounded too loud in her ears. She felt Brandon Marsh's eyes on her. While everyone else was looking at him, he was looking at her.

"Oh, I don't know. Let's say five dollars."

"Oh, yes, well in that case..."

Somehow she worked her way through the customers ahead of him, each one of whom had something to say that had little to do with the transaction, but more to do with local gossip, until he was finally at the counter. His arms were folded over his chest and he was staring at her, his dark eyebrows drawn together in a puzzled frown. He was better looking at second glance—or was it third glance—with high cheekbones, deep-set eyes and a square jaw.

"What are you doing here?" he asked. A hush fell over the small office as everyone else in line stopped talking to listen to the tall, handsome stranger interact with their assistant postmistress.

"I work here. I'm the assistant postmistress. Someday soon I hope to be the actual postmistress," she said. Though why she felt the need to communicate her career plans to a stranger, she didn't know. She was just afraid of allowing a moment of silence between them. "Anyway, I'm sorry, but the mail hasn't been sorted yet. I know I told you two o'clock, but I've been so busy...."

"Are you all alone here?" he asked, looking behind her.

"Yes. This is not exactly San Francisco. This is Silverado. We don't have all that much business. Well, actually we have enough to keep me busy selling stamps and mailing packages and sorting mail."

"Yes, I see."

What was wrong with her? He knew what post office employees did. She didn't have to explain as if he'd never been in one before.

"Shall I come back another time?" he asked.

"If you don't mind. It's been so busy today...."

"I know. You said that."

She blushed. She'd been working there for the past year and a half. She rarely got rattled, no matter how many people were in line, but today she couldn't seem to get organized. It was the move. Then it was Dylan and now it was this man.

"I'll be back," he said, and turned and walked out the door.

The atmosphere in the room changed the minute he left. Customers resumed their conversations. After craning their necks to stare at the stranger, they went back to making small talk as they waited their turn. When she finally got a break, she went to the back room and dumped the leather sack of mail onto her small desk, sat down and began to sort briskly through the envelopes and packages, hoping to get through them before he came back.

But she didn't. She glanced up to find him looming in the doorway.

"Don't mind me," he said.

She nodded. But she did mind him. She tried to ignore him, this disturbing newcomer. She tried to stack the mail into neat piles. But his gray gaze was so unnerving, she found she'd put the *A*'s in with the *C*'s and the *Z*'s with the *S*'s. She'd have to resort it later, after he left. The sooner the better.

"You might want to get a cup of coffee at the coffee shop," she suggested. "I'm still not finished." Anything to get rid of him.

"I don't need coffee, I need food. How's the food there?"

"Probably not up to your standards."

"How do you know what my standards are?" he asked.

"I know you're from San Francisco."

"Is the coffee shop the only place in town to eat?" he asked.

"There's the diner, but..."

"Don't tell me. It's not up to my standards, either."

She shrugged. "There's my aunt's bed-and-breakfast."

"What good would that do? I have a bed and I make my own breakfast," he said.

"She may branch out into dinners."

"Is she a good cook?"

"Yes, very, but..."

"But it's only for guests. I understand." Brandon braced his arms against the door frame. He wanted to go back to the ranch, but he had no desire to thaw something from the gigantic freezer that he'd filled from his supermarket trip on his way to town. He was hungry, impatient and anxious to see his mail. At the rate this postmistress, former owner of his ranch, was going, it would be dark before he got back on the road.

"Can I help you with that?" he asked, his eyes on a large envelope he knew was his.

"It's against government regulations," she said stiffly. "I'm almost finished."

"Are we going to go through this every day?" he asked. This was not the way he pictured his life on a Nevada ranch. Standing around the post office waiting for his mail. Watching an attractive postmistress weed through the letters. And she *was* attractive. In her own way. Not his type though, with her lack of makeup and wild hairstyle. If you could call it a style.

She stood and handed him a stack of letters. Her hand brushed his. Slender fingers, soft skin. His gaze met hers, then she looked away quickly.

A strange sensation hit him under his ribs. A shock. A recognition of something out of the ordinary. He tried to ignore it by shuffling through the envelopes, extracting the one he was waiting for and slitting it open. His heart pounded when he saw the legal letterhead. He scanned the words that traveled across the page. The man who was responsible for killing his family had been released from jail.

The blood drained out of Brandon's head. He'd never passed out but he knew how it would feel. Just like this.

"Are you all right?" she asked. Her voice came from far away. Concerned, anxious.

"Fine. I think I'll have that cup of coffee now."

He stood outside the post office and filled his lungs with fresh air. There was a small, dirty boy leaning against his car, running the wheels of a plastic car over the hood.

"Hey," he shouted. Startled, the boy jumped a foot in the air. Brandon dropped his mail and the kid's plastic car went flying, hit the sidewalk and split into a dozen pieces onto the pavement.

"You broke my car," Dylan cried.

"I didn't break your car, but you scratched mine," Brandon said, examining the deep scratches in the mirror-smooth hood of his new car.

"What happened?" Laura McIntyre was standing in front of the post office in her trim navy skirt and white crisp blouse, her hands on her hips.

"Nothing. It's all right. It doesn't matter," Brandon said.

Laura strode up to the car and bent over the hood. "Did you do this?" she asked the boy.

"I was just playing. Pretending it was mine." He hung his head.

"I'm sorry about this, Mr. Marsh," she said. "Naturally I'll pay for the repair."

"That won't be necessary."

"Yes, it will. I insist."

He shrugged. If she wanted to pay for it, let her. The woman shifted her glance from the hood of the car to her son and back to the car. Her shoulders slumped and he was afraid she was going to cry. Her son was staring at his scuffed shoes. Brandon felt a pang of unwanted sympathy for both of them.

"Never mind," he said brusquely. "Forget it."

He got into his car and drove back to the ranch. Where no one could scratch the surface of his car or his heart.

"WHAT IS WRONG with you?" Laura asked, holding her son by the shoulders. "That is an expensive car. It's going to cost an awful lot to get the scratch out of the finish."

He shrugged.

"And whatever it is, it's more than we can afford. Do you understand that?"

He nodded, but kept his head down.

"What were you doing?"

"Playing," he mumbled.

She sighed loudly. "I have to go back to work now, but I'll discuss this with you later. I want you to go back to Aunt Emily's and stay there until I get there. Do you hear me?"

He nodded. He heard her. But instead of walking down the street in the direction of the bed-and-breakfast, he stooped down and scooped up the pieces of his plastic car, one by one, and put them in his pocket. Then he turned and walked away in the opposite direction without speaking another word to her. Even a complaint would have been better than his silence. Even the question about his father, as painful as it was, would have been better. As she watched him trudge away, her eyes filled with tears. She wished she hadn't been so harsh; she wished he'd turn around and say something. Like where he was going. Anything would be better than nothing.

She had to find something constructive for him to do this summer. But what? She couldn't afford a baby-sitter every day, and even if she could, he'd already declared he was too old for one. He was too young for summer school. Too rambunctious to leave at home and too unpredictable to let loose.

She'd hoped that between her aunt and herself they

could keep an eye on him, but it wasn't working out that way. She didn't know what the solution was. Her dream of being a stay-at-home mom was fading to nothing.

She sighed and glanced up at the notice on the wall for the postmistress job. As if that would solve all of her problems. It wouldn't, but it would be a start. She had to admit she was counting on the job. Although anyone at all could apply for it, she was sure she'd get it. Who else would apply? Who would want to live in Silverado? And who among the residents would qualify except herself?

Yes, she had to have that job. She had to have the salary increase and she had to have this small apartment above the post office now occupied by Willa Mae, the current postmistress who was on the verge of retirement. It was going to be the new home she'd promised Dylan. It wasn't a ranch. But she'd make it into a home for them. She had to. In between waiting on customers she thought of how she'd redecorate, even rebuild the tree house behind the building, and the afternoon flew by.

THAT NIGHT she followed her aunt's recipe and cooked a coq au vin for six without her aunt's help. Not that Aunt Em didn't want to help. But after one look at her ashen face, Laura insisted she stay in bed. Fortunately she had Dylan for a sous chef. Whether he was trying to make amends for his behavior that afternoon over the car incident, or he realized how much she needed him, he rose to the occasion. Without complaining and with her supervision, he set the table, carried dishes in and out of the high-ceilinged dining room and took out the garbage afterward.

When he got a five-dollar tip he was proud and ecstatic.

"Can I keep it?" he asked, studying the picture of Abraham Lincoln on the greenback.

"Of course you can. You earned it. You worked hard tonight."

"I could buy another model car or—" he wrinkled his nose "—or I could give it to the guy with the car to help pay for the...you know."

She hugged him, feeling her heart swell with pride. If she weren't so dog-tired she would have jumped for joy. The moment she'd been waiting for had arrived. Dylan was coming around. First he'd worked without complaining for the past hour. He'd actually taken her suggestions without a murmur. He hadn't mentioned his father, and now he was showing remorse and a willingness to make amends. Of course he hadn't actually said he was sorry, but just volunteering to part with his hard-earned money was more than she'd expected and a good sign that this stubborn phase of his life might be finally coming to an end. And not a moment too soon.

The next morning Laura walked to work with a lighter step. Her aunt was up and in the kitchen stirring up waffles, looking tired but determined. She said she was not going to stay in bed another minute, despite Laura's offer to cook breakfast for the guests. Laura would have insisted, but she had a sneaking suspicion that Aunt Em didn't think her cooking was up to her standards. After all, she considered herself a professional chef and her niece, though talented, was just an amateur.

At lunch Laura ran over the rules with Dylan once again and he didn't even protest. Now all she needed to do to get her life back on track was to nail down that job. That very afternoon a representative from the personnel office of the central post office was due to visit her branch. The next step would be the interview, and then she was in. At least she hoped so. By all rights she should have the job. She'd been working there ever since Willa Mae, the longtime postmistress, went on medical leave.

Willa Mae had just recently announced her retirement after forty years in the post office, and had made plans to leave Silverado and go live with her sister. Everyone assumed Laura would get the job. And the apartment. It was the next step on Laura's way to independence. Both financial and emotional.

At exactly 4:55 that afternoon, when the post office was bursting at the seams with the last-minute customers as well as the official from the post office who'd come to interview her, the phone rang.

"Mrs. McIntyre, your son is on my property," Brandon Marsh said angrily. "He's sitting in a tree house and he won't come down. He says he's waiting for his daddy to come back."

Her knees buckled. She gripped the edge of the counter. He couldn't...he wouldn't...but he had. "Oh, no."

"Oh, yes. I suggest you come and get him."

"Can I talk to him?"

"As far as I know, there's no phone in the tree house," he said.

"I know, but..." She glanced at the clock. "I—I'll be there as soon as I can." Just as soon as she closed up and had her interview. Surely he could wait that long.

BRANDON STOOD under the tall, rickety, homemade ladder that led to the tree house and stared up at the worn soles of a pair of dirty sneakers.

"Come down from that tree right now," he ordered.

"No. I'm not coming down till my daddy comes back." There was no mistaking the determination in his voice. Brandon had no idea how to deal with a stubborn eight-year-old. He didn't usually avoid problems. But he always avoided eight-year-olds. And kids of all ages. On the other hand, he found most other kinds of problems challenging. But not this messy kind of personal problem. He wanted to go back in the house and study a spread sheet he had on his computer. So he could solve a problem for a Silicon Valley start-up he was consulting for. A problem he could deal with coolly and efficiently and impersonally.

At one time in his life, a long time ago, he wouldn't have minded a boy in his tree house. He would have built the house himself. And invited the boy to help. But not now. If things had been different...if his child had had a chance to grow up... But he hadn't.

Dylan stood and leaned over the railing which made an ominous creaking sound. His eyes widened in alarm and he stepped back from the edge.

"Would you get down here right now," Brandon said. Where was the kid's mother? What was wrong with her that she couldn't control her son? If he had a son... But he didn't. Not anymore.

Dylan shook his head. Was it Brandon's imagination or did the whole wooden platform shake, too? All he needed was to have the kid fall out of the tree and break his arm. Kids were so fragile. One minute they were talking, laughing, riding in a car over slick streets, and the next minute... The worst thing was they didn't know it. They thought they were invincible.

Maybe that was the best way. To live life fearlessly. As if you had some control over the outcome. Until one day you learned you had no control at all and you found out how quickly life could be snuffed out. How irrevocably things could change forever. This tree house appeared to be falling apart before his very eyes. Whoever built it had obviously thrown it together, and it wasn't meant to last. He just hoped it would last until his mother arrived. Or his father.

"When is your daddy coming back?" Brandon asked.

"Pretty soon."

"Where did he go?"

"He went to the moon on a spaceship."

"So he's an astronaut," Brandon said.

"Yeah, that's right. He's gonna bring me back some moon rocks and a saddle and a video game. But I gotta wait for him right here until he comes back."

"You can't wait here. It's not safe. Look, kid, whatever your name is..."

"Dylan," came the muffled voice.

"Be reasonable, Dylan. You don't live here anymore. Why would your father come here to look for you?"

"Cuz this is where his spaceship lands."

Brandon looked around at the meadow that surrounded the tree. He had to admit this would be an ideal spot for a spaceship to land. But he wasn't going to admit that to the boy. He braced his hand against the rough bark and looked up. "Your mother's on her way. You don't want to make her wait for you, do you?"

"You shouldna' told her I was here," he said, "cuz I'm not going back with her. I'm staying here." He stomped one foot on the platform for emphasis.

The whole structure shook. Dylan grabbed a limb of the tree. Brandon held his arms out to catch the kid, as if he could save him. He hadn't been able to save his own son, so why would he be able to save some one else's boy? The tree house was falling apart, and once it did, there'd be no putting it together again. He was sure the boy would come hurtling down in a minute. But the boards held and nothing happened. Brandon heaved a sigh of relief.

"Are you still mad at me?" Dylan asked.

"For putting a scratch in my car? I'm not happy about it."

"My mom says I gotta pay to get it fixed. I already got five dollars."

"That's a start. Why don't you come down and maybe we can work something out."

"No. I told you—"

"I know what you told me. Look, what if your dad is stuck on the moon for a while and he can't get back anytime soon? If he comes when you're gone, I'll tell him you've moved."

"He won't believe you."

Oh, Lord, this was one stubborn kid. How in the hell was he going to get him out of the tree? He leaned against the trunk. He wanted to walk away. To go into the house, close the door behind him and forget about this kid and his sad-eyed mother and his astronaut father and the furniture he left in his room.

"Hey, you forgot your Legos? Why don't you come up and see if there's anything else you forgot?"

"Like what?"

"Like...maybe baseball cards or...I don't know."

"How much did your car cost?" the boy asked, peering over the edge of the platform. "Seventy thousand?"

"No, not that much."

"My dad's gonna get one like that, or maybe more expensive, like a Porsche. He's coming to get me in it."

"What about the spaceship? Never mind. You like cars?"

Dylan nodded. "Fast cars."

A truck coughed and sputtered in his driveway. She was here. At last. Thank God.

Dylan heard it, too. He moved back into the partial shelter of what was intended to be an A-frame tree house.

"Hey, come on down," Brandon yelled. "Your mom's here."

"I'm not coming down. She'll be mad at me."

"She'll be even madder if you don't come down."

Brandon watched Laura McIntyre marched purposefully across the field in her regulation post office uniform with crisp white shirt and sensible navy blue midheels. The late-afternoon sun picked up copper streaks in her dark hair. She looked mad enough to haul her son home with her and punish him severely. Which was exactly what she ought to do. And about time. He had to learn to obey her. Stay out of trees.

Stay out of danger. He knew he'd hate to be in her way when she had that look in her eyes.

She ignored Brandon as if he wasn't there. Her whole attention was focused on her son.

"Dylan, get down here this minute."

"No, I don't hafta. I'm not going back with you. I'm waiting."

"He's waiting for his father to pick him up," Brandon explained.

"I know what he's waiting for," she said stiffly. She tilted her head back to regard her son. "All right, I'm coming up to get you."

"I wouldn't recommend that, Mrs. McIntyre," Brandon said. "And I wouldn't recommend making threats you can't follow through on."

"Thank you very much for your advice. Who are you anyway—Dr. Spock? Do you think I can't climb this tree, Mr. Marsh?" she demanded, turning to look at him for the first time. He felt the full force of her blazing eyes, her anger and her frustration.

"I'm sure you can. I just don't recommend it. And for God's sake, would you quit calling me Mr. Marsh? My name is Brandon."

"Then stop calling me Mrs. McIntrye. My name is Laura. What exactly do you recommend I do, *Brandon,* if you know so much about child psychology?" she said.

She had him there. "Nothing," he said, the muscles in his jaw tightening. "I don't know anything about psychology and even less about children. So you handle it yourself. Good luck." He rested his hands on his hips and stared at her. This was the moment when he would be completely justified in walking back to his house and closing the door behind him. But he no longer wanted to retreat into his house. He knew he wouldn't be able to think about anything but this woman and her son. He was too curious. He wanted to see how she was going to manage this situation. If she was going to manage it.

She stared back at him. Lord, he was maddening. She kicked off her shoes, grasped the rungs of the ladder and started to climb up in her narrow, hip-hugging, knee-length skirt.

He steadied the ladder. Looking up, he had a glimpse of long, smooth legs that didn't quit, a lace slip and panties to match. He felt a sudden dizziness, as if he was the one in danger of falling off a wobbly platform twenty feet above the ground, instead of the one gripping the ladder with both hands.

What was wrong with him? He hadn't looked at a woman for two years. And he hadn't looked up a woman's skirt since he was on the junior high play-ground. But now he stood there watching her firm rounded bottom stretch the confines of her narrow skirt and her lace underwear, and waiting for her to fall into his arms.

Chapter Three

''Don't come up,'' Dylan shouted to his mother. ''This is my house. Private. Keep out.''

Halfway up the shaky ladder, Laura hesitated. If he wouldn't come down voluntarily, how could she force him, either physically or verbally? She couldn't. Not twenty feet off the ground. Uncertain what to do next, she looked down over her shoulder and met the gaze of the owner of her land. He was staring up at her with an intensity that startled her so much she almost lost her grip.

A wave of dizziness hit her. So this was vertigo. She'd never been afraid of heights before, but she was now. She was afraid of falling. Falling into his outstretched arms.

''Don't look down,'' he yelled.

She wrenched her gaze from his, stared straight ahead at the bark of the tree and put one foot down, then the next, one rung at a time until her feet hit solid ground. She stumbled and Brandon grabbed her by both arms. She fell backward against his chest.

''Don't you know any better than to climb a tree if you're afraid of heights?'' he demanded.

She jerked out of his grasp, startled by the rocklike

muscles that she'd encountered and by the way her pulse raced. Bending down, she grabbed her shoes. "I'm not afraid of heights," she said.

"You could have fooled me."

"I've climbed this tree a hundred times."

"Recently?"

"When I was a child."

"You're not a child anymore." His cool gray gaze assessed her, traveling from the top of her head, down her wrinkled uniform to the low-heeled shoes she'd slipped into. She shifted her weight from one foot to the other. Damn, he was making her uncomfortable. He made her even more uncomfortable when he reached over and removed an oak leaf from where it was tangled in her hair. Just the touch of his hand surprised and disturbed her.

"Thank you," she said breathlessly.

"For what?"

"Holding the ladder." She'd just realized that while Brandon had been holding the ladder for her he'd presumably gotten a good look up her skirt. If he'd cared to look, which he probably hadn't.

He shrugged. "Coming down was a wise decision."

"I wish I could convince my son of that." She rubbed her forehead with the back of her hand. What now? She was stuck between a rock and a hard place. The rock was her son—and the hard place? The man next to her who looked like he'd do anything to get rid of them.

She swallowed hard. "I'm really sorry about this."

"Not any sorrier than I am."

"You must think I can't control my own son."

''Can you?''

''Of course. I'm just going to give him a few minutes to reconsider. When he realizes he has no choice...''

''He's waiting for his father to come and get him,'' Brandon repeated.

''You said that,'' she said stiffly ''It's not going to happen.''

Brandon didn't say anything. Unlike most people, he didn't ask why not, or where he was, or when he was coming back. He just stood there gazing off in the distance across the timeless land to the magnificent mountains in the far distance.

''It's a nice view,'' she said, following his gaze. ''My father always called it God's country.''

''Your family owned this land for some time I understand,'' he said.

She nodded. ''Four generations. I thought we always would, but—'' She stopped abruptly. She'd cried enough over the loss of the land. This was not the time. Not in front of the new owner. She didn't want pity. Especially not his pity. She took a deep breath. ''My great-grandfather came by wagon train. On his way to the gold fields in California. He never meant to stop in Nevada, but his wagon broke down, he lost his team and he never made it over the Sierra Nevada.''

''Bad luck,'' Brandon said sympathetically.

''Not entirely. While he was looking for his lost mules, up there in the mountain behind our ranch, he accidentally stumbled over an outcrop of a greenish ore that looked worthless but turned out to contain silver. Enough so he could buy up all this land, build a house and send for my great-grandmother back in St. Louis. He chose well.''

''You mean your great-grandmother or the land?''

She smiled. ''Both. Great-Grandmother Kimpton was a city girl, but she adjusted beautifully. Started the first school in Silverado and even taught there. As for the land, Great-Grandpa saw the springs in the mountain up there when he was prospecting. He knew the value of water in this high desert, so he channeled it and later my dad dammed up the stream and built the reservoir. Which is the story in a nutshell of why we've been here ever since. I mean, we *had been* here ever since.''

How long would it take to get it through her head that she didn't live here anymore? That it wasn't McIntyre land any longer. That a dynasty was over. She brushed her hands together briskly. Trying not to think of her ancestors who'd built and planted and worked the land so she could have a life here, so she could leave it to her children. What would they think? What would they say?

Brandon stared off into the mountains as if he was picturing her great-grandfather, looking for his mule, stumbling over silver.

''Dylan will be down in a few minutes,'' she said to break the awkward silence. ''I know he will. It's almost dinnertime and he'll be hungry. Then we'll be gone. I promise you. Don't feel you have to stay out here. You have—you must have things to do. What are you planning to use the land for? Raise livestock, or—''

''No.''

''I see,'' she said. But she didn't see. What on earth did he want all this land for, enough to pay an outrageous sum for it, if he didn't intend to use it for something? "The rumor in town is you're going to turn it into a theme park."

His mouth twitched as if he might smile or even laugh. For some reason she wished he would. She'd like to see what he looked like with a smile on his face. But he didn't.

"A theme park," he mused with mock seriousness. "There's an idea. What would the theme be?"

"I don't know. Maybe a silver mining camp, with an elevator to the bottom of a mine shaft and shovels for the kids," she speculated.

"Where a visitor might possibly find some more of that greenish ore stuff and get to keep it. Is that what you suggest?" he asked.

"Not me," she protested, annoyed at the mocking tone in his voice. "I'm certainly not suggesting you build a theme park of any kind. But if you did, at least it would be historically accurate."

"Didn't they have gunfights and a saloon on every corner?" he asked.

"My grandpa had a gun." Dylan's voice came wafting down from the tree house where he'd obviously been listening to their whole conversation. "Kept it locked in his gun cabinet. I'm gonna get one, too, when my daddy comes back." Laura jerked her head up and Brandon looked up at the same time. For a moment she'd almost forgotten he was up there.

"Dylan," she called. "Come down, please."

No answer. She sighed loudly.

"Dylan," Brandon yelled. "If you come down we'll go for a ride in my car."

"Please don't promise him anything you can't deliver," she said softly.

"At this point I'm ready to deliver almost anything, if he'll come down out of that tree. It's not safe, you know."

She nodded and glanced nervously up at the tree. After a long moment Dylan poked his head out of the door of the tree house. "How fast does it go?" he asked.

"A hundred twenty," Brandon shouted.

Laura gasped. "You're not taking him out on the road to break the speed limit."

"We won't go over seventy," he promised. "Isn't it worth it to get the kid out of the tree?"

"I—I don't know."

"You can work the sunroof," Brandon called.

"What about the stereo?" the boy asked.

He shrugged.

"All right."

They watched him climb down the ladder, his feet flying agilely down the rungs.

"Let's go," Dylan said.

"That all right with you?" Brandon asked Laura.

As if she had a choice at that point. It was either Dylan go for a ride in the speed demon's car or go back up the tree.

"I guess so."

She stood in the driveway as they pulled away, listening to the stereo blaring, watching the sunroof opening and closing and opening again. She hadn't seen Dylan so excited for months. Ever since Jason left, he'd been a different child from the one she'd given birth to. His natural joy, his love of life was dimmed like a hurricane lamp running out of oil.

She was encouraged but worried at the same time. She didn't know why exactly. Driving seventy miles an hour on a deserted Nevada highway wasn't exactly unheard of. Dylan would be wearing a seat belt. He'd had that drummed into him. It was just...this man and her son...

She paced back and forth in the driveway. Waiting...watching. After long minutes ticked by she walked around to the back of the house to her herb garden. The pungent smells of sage, oregano and basil filled the air. She plucked a sprig of lavender and crushed it between her fingers. She missed her house, her view and her horse, but most of all she missed her herb garden. Her refuge, her haven, her escape from her troubles these past few years.

Every fall she picked the herbs, then retreated to the potting shed where she hung them from the ceiling to dry and packed them away for winter. This year there would be no harvest. They'd wither and die without water. Knowing it would be her last chance, she sprayed the dry earth with the hose attached to the outdoor faucet.

"There you go," she told the plants. "This one's on me. Come on, drink up. It may be your last."

"We're back."

She whirled around to see Brandon standing in front of a rosemary plant that had gone to seed and turned into a bush.

"Oh, good," she said, "you're back." Inadvertently she clenched her fist around the hose handle. Water spurted from the nozzle, soaking him from head to foot. He jumped out of the way, but it was too late. His dark hair hung in damp strands on his forehead. The water dripped off his chin. His wet pants molded to the muscles of his thighs and his shirt stuck to his chest. He stood there staring at her so stoically, she gave in to an irrepressible urge to laugh. She laughed so hard she couldn't stop. She was on the edge of hysteria. Tired, worried, tense, she felt like she was coming apart at the seams.

"It wasn't *that* funny," he said.

She took a deep breath before she spoke and struggled to regain her composure. He must think she was an idiot. "I know. I'm sorry."

Impulsively she reached out and brushed the water off the front of his shirt. His chest was solid and muscular under his wet shirt. Startled at the way her heart rate sped up just from the physical contact with a stranger, the second time today, she dropped her hand as fast as if she'd been burned.

"Who were you talking to when I got here?" he asked, apparently oblivious to the effect he had on her.

"No one. Where's Dylan?" she asked anxiously.

"He's still sitting in the car, opening and closing the windows. And testing the air conditioning."

"Aren't you afraid...?" she said.

"Yes, I'm afraid he'll never leave."

"I'll get him," she said, taking a step around him. "Thank you for doing what you did. I appreciate it. Sometimes it's hard, raising a child without..." She trailed off, embarrassed to be caught admitting to having problems. To being a single parent. Admitting anything negative to anyone at all, especially this man.

"Don't thank me," he said blocking her way. "Do me a favor. Send someone to tear down the tree house and get rid of these weeds."

"But..."

"Naturally I'll pay for it. I just don't know who to call."

"They're not weeds. This is my herb garden."

"Whatever. I don't want an herb garden. I don't want any garden, and I don't want a tree house. The next thing you know your son will be back up the tree, and this time we won't be here to catch him or coax him down and he'll fall out of it. I can't take a chance like that."

"No. I won't let him come back. This is the last time, I promise you. But please don't take down the tree house. Not yet. It doesn't mean anything to you, but it's all he has."

"Then take it with you."

Dylan came running through the garden out of nowhere and threw himself against Brandon like a whirling dervish, pounding him with his fists. "You're not gonna tear it down," he yelled. "And we're not gonna take it with us. It's gonna stay here until my daddy comes back. And so am I."

With that, the boy turned and raced around the house, with Laura and Brandon following close behind. He raced across the driveway and scrambled up the ladder once again, two steps at a time, and flung himself into the tree house while they watched helplessly from below. A silence fell over the meadow, broken only by the slight breeze that ruffled the leaves. Or was that the sound of a boy's muffled sobs? Laura stood staring up at the tree house, shoulders slumped, only vaguely aware of the man next to her, whom she was sure oozed disapproval from her lack of control over her son.

"Well?" he said.

"Well," she said, "I'm not going up after him."

"A wise decision," he said brusquely. "Considering the condition of the steps and your inability to climb them."

She glared at him and bit her tongue to keep from blurting that it was his fault Dylan was back in the tree house. If he hadn't threatened to tear down the jerry-built structure... "My inability to climb the tree has nothing to do with it, nor the condition of the ladder. It's the principle, my approach to parenting that's the reason. I don't expect you to understand, not being a parent yourself."

He stared at her with an expression as stunned as if she'd slapped him across the face. His mouth opened as if to say something, to put her in her place, as she'd try to do to him, but he never said a word. He snapped his mouth closed, and without speaking, he turned on his heel and marched off in the direction of the house, leaving her feeling like she'd done something terrible, but she had no idea what. Whatever it was, she had no time to worry about him.

Her son was hurt, angry and up a tree, and she had no idea of how to get him down. Despite her brave words, and her bluster about child psychology, she didn't know what to do next except to wait. She would wait there until he came down and then they'd go home. How long could he stay up there, waiting for his father, after all? As she'd told Brandon, he would get hungry, he would get discouraged, he would see reason. After all, he was a reasonable kid and he'd soon realize there was no point in staying up there and come down. They'd drive home, they'd have dinner with Aunt Emily... Aunt Emily. Aunt Emily was expecting them for dinner along with her guests. Laura had promised to make the salad. It was almost six o'clock and she'd be worried, she'd be wondering…

"Dylan," Laura shouted, "come down here this minute or I'm coming up to get you." His words echoed in her head. *I wouldn't recommend making threats you can't carry through on.*

Silence.

"Did you hear me?" she asked.

"Not coming down," came a muffled voice.

She looked at her watch and sighed loudly. Now what? Dylan wouldn't come down and she *shouldn't, wouldn't, couldn't* go up. Even if she did go up, she couldn't force him to come down. So what was the point?

"All right," she said. "Stay up there then. I'm going—I'm going to make a phone call and I'll be right back."

No answer. She backed away from the tree, her eyes on the tree house, watching for a movement, listening for a sound from him. Hoping against hope he'd come down now. Because if there was anything she didn't want to do, it was to visit her old house and intrude on Brandon Marsh. Not after seeing the look on his face when she'd lectured him on her approach to parenting. She dreaded even asking him to use his phone. He'd made it abundantly clear he didn't want to be disturbed. But how disturbing could it be to take a moment to make a phone call?

She couldn't shake the thought of her aunt leaning over the stove, stirring her sauce, listening for the sound of Laura's truck, then instead of joining the guests in the living room for sherry and hors d'oeuvres, she'd have to start tearing lettuce and chopping vegetables for her salad, the one Laura had promised to make for her, her forehead puckered with worry lines. Aunt Emily was under doctor's orders not to worry. Laura turned her back to the tree house and ran to the ranch house and knocked on the front door. There was no answer. She knocked again. Louder. He had to be there. His car was in the driveway.

She tried to turn the knob. It didn't budge. She knocked again. No answer. She peered in the window. The living room was exactly the way she'd left it—could it be only a few days ago? Not a sign that anyone had moved in. The same chairs flanking the fireplace at exactly the same angle, the ones she'd chosen the fabric to recover, the pictures on the wall that had hung there for twenty years or more. Wasn't he going to change anything?

Desperate, she knocked louder. What if Dylan had come down and was looking for her? What if her aunt had called the sheriff's office to report her missing? She pressed her shoulder against the door and looked over her shoulder in the direction of the tree house, just in case. When Brandon opened the door she lurched forward into the room. She gasped in surprise as he caught her in his arms before she fell. Two things registered—he'd changed into a dry shirt and pants and he smelled like leather and expensive shaving lotion. For the third time that evening she'd come into intimate physical contact with this man and this time, not only did her heart race, her knees buckled.

"No one ever locks their doors," she blurted, jerking backward, hoping he couldn't see her cheeks flame with embarrassment.

"Is that so?" Obviously, by the dour tone of his voice, having a woman fall into his arms had no effect on him, while her heart was going a mile a minute.

"They even leave their car keys in the ignition," she added. "You're in the country now."

"Thank you for that information. Now if that's all..."

"No, no, it isn't. I came to use your phone just for a moment, if I may."

"Can I assume your son is still in the tree?"

"Yes, he is. But he'll be down soon. Any minute. I promise I won't bother you again if I can make one phone call. You see, my aunt expects us for dinner and it's getting late and..."

Brandon reached into his back pocket and pulled out the smallest cell phone she'd ever seen. Wordlessly he handed it to her.

"Thank you." She punched in the numbers with fumbling fingers. He made her nervous, standing there staring at her. Since he seemed to have every intention of staying right there and listening to her conversation, she'd make it brief.

"Aunt Emily, I'm sorry I'm late, but..."

"What happened?" her aunt asked anxiously. "I've been worried about you."

"No, no, you mustn't worry about me. I'm fine. Everything's fine. I'm out at the ranch."

"The ranch? Why? Where's Dylan?"

"He's here, too."

"But how did that happen? What are you doing there?"

She glanced at Brandon, who was standing at the window looking out at the shadows falling over the meadow, his arms crossed over his chest, his expression void of any interest in her conversation, almost as if she wasn't there, which he probably wished she wasn't. On the other hand, he might be taking in every word she said, processing it and finding her lacking for one reason or another.

"It's a long story, Aunt Em," Laura said patiently.

"Does it have something to do with the new owner?" her aunt asked eagerly.

"No. Not at all," Laura said firmly.

"Too bad," her aunt murmured. "But he is there, isn't he?"

"Yes," Laura admitted.

"I happened to hear some news about him today when I ran into Buzz, the Realtor, in the bank."

"Oh? Well, I won't keep you, Aunt Em. Don't worry, I'll be back in time to toss the salad."

"No, no, I've already taken care of it. Don't hurry home," the older lady instructed. "You just stay there until you do whatever it is you have to do."

"All right, if you're sure," Laura said with relief. After all, she had no idea how long it would take to get Dylan out of the tree. She said goodbye and handed the phone back to Brandon.

"And now I'll get out of your way," she said, and turned toward the door.

"So everything's fine," he said, a trace of sarcasm in his voice. So he had been listening to her conversation. "What are you going to do?" he asked.

"I'm going out to wait," she said. As if he cared.

"How long?" he asked.

"As long as it takes," she said, turning to face him. "Look, I'm sorry that once again I've intruded. You've made it quite clear you don't want me or my son around and I don't blame you. It's your house and you're entitled to your privacy. It's just...it's just..." She swallowed hard and forced herself to continue. She wouldn't play the role of the female in distress; she wouldn't.

Just because she'd lost her husband and her farm, she still had her dignity. A few shreds of it. Or she had had it before today. Before she'd been forced to come back to her home as an interloper, forced to beg to stay long enough to coax her son to return home with her. Home. Where was home? How could she blame an eight-year-old for not understanding that he had no home anymore, that a stranger had taken it over. A stranger with a lot of money and nobody to share it with. Or did he?

She took a deep breath. "I'll be gone just as soon as I get Dylan down. I'll be very quiet. You won't even know I'm out there," she said. She hesitated a moment, expecting him to make another caustic remark about her or Dylan, but he only shrugged, so she walked out into the dusk without another word.

She used to love this time of day on the ranch. As the cattle came meandering back to the barn in the evening, Dylan would come in from his tree house or the rubber tire swing under the oak tree and Jason would join them from his office where he was wheeling and dealing some business deal.

That was then, this was now. The ranch had dwindled to almost half its original size. And it wasn't even hers. Her family was down to the two of them. She and Dylan. He was all she had. Except for her aunt. Thank heavens for Aunt Em. Despite her busybody manner, her nose for gossip and her eagerness to find Laura a good husband this time around, she was as good-hearted as they came. She truly wanted the best for Laura, and the best included another husband.

Aunt Emily couldn't get it through her head that Laura's future was decided and it didn't include another marriage. Her future revolved around supporting herself and her son. She always knew it wouldn't be easy to leave the ranch. She had no idea it would involve sitting at the foot of the old oak tree, her back against the rough bark, hungry and tired, waiting for her son who was waiting for his daddy to come back.

BRANDON HAD WORK to do. His goal in moving to the ranch was not to cut himself off from his clients; it was to cut himself off from well-meaning friends. But tonight his clients and his work were the farthest thing from his mind. All he could think about was that woman and her son out there in the tree. He couldn't relax until they'd left. Which hadn't happened yet. He'd know if they'd gone, because her truck's engine made such a God-awful noise. That vehicle was a disaster waiting to happen.

That meant the kid was still there, up the tree, and the woman was begging, coaxing, threatening—whatever it took—to get him down. She was right. He didn't know anything about parenting. If he had, he wouldn't have lost his own son. He would have stopped Jeanne from taking him out in the car that foggy day. He knew instinctively it was too dangerous. But Jeanne laughed off his fears and went anyway. She'd been strong-willed. Knew exactly what she wanted. She'd wanted him and she'd wanted a baby.

So he didn't know anything about parenting. But he knew that it was dinnertime and the kid had to be hungry. And as much as he didn't want to see the woman again, he couldn't stand there doing nothing when he knew she and her son were on his property. Brandon didn't have much in the large, old-fashioned pantry or in the freezer. Only the supplies he'd stocked up on at the supermarket on the highway on his way to town, but maybe the boy could be tempted by a peanut-butter sandwich. At this moment, it even sounded good to Brandon. He went to the kitchen and made three sandwiches on whole-grain bread. Before he could change his mind, he piled them on a paper plate and walked out the front door, leaving it not only unlocked, but wide open. Point taken. He was in the country now.

When he saw her there, sitting on the ground, her arms around her knees, her face hidden by her dark hair, his gut tightened with an unfamiliar emotion. It was part sympathy for her plight, part annoyance at her stubbornness, part admiration for her determination and something else. Something that was buried deep inside him. Something he was afraid to probe any further to discover. Something that caused him to be more brusque than he'd intended.

"Not down yet." It was a statement, not a question. If he'd come down, they'd be gone. Obviously.

She looked up, and even in the gathering dusk he could see the faint lines in her forehead deepen, notice smudges under her eyes. He had a wild, crazy desire to smooth those wrinkles, to erase those smudges. Where was Dylan's father when he needed him, when she needed a man? He could hear her take a deep breath and see her make a visible effort to pull herself together. He hardened his heart. She didn't want sympathy from him and truthfully, he had none to give. He was hollow inside, stripped bare of any remaining emotion.

"No, but any minute..." she said hopefully.

"You said he'd get hungry." He held out the plate. "I thought maybe a sandwich might encourage him."

She stood and brushed off the seat of her skirt with one hand and took the paper plate with the other. "Thank you. That's very...but I...I don't know. I've been calling him, but he hasn't made a sound since I came back."

Brandon looked up at the tree house. No shoes hanging over the edge of the platform. "Mind if I try?" he asked.

"Go ahead."

"Dylan, come on down and have a peanut-butter sandwich with us." It might have been his imagination, but he thought he detected a slight movement in the tree house, a faint creaking of the boards. Laura met his gaze and he saw a flicker of hope in her eyes.

There was a long silence. Then another sound. This time it was definitely a creaking board. Then thumping. The boy was on his feet, his chin on the rickety railing, his arms dangling over the railing. Brandon glanced at Laura. Her eyes were wide, but she wasn't as frightened as Brandon was. He knew how fast accidents happen. He knew that a life can be snuffed out in seconds. Just one false step. Just one careless act. She didn't know that. She'd never lost a son.

"No. If I come down you'll tear my tree house down."

"Not now. Not until we have a deal," Brandon said.

"What kind of a deal?"

Brandon exhaled loudly. How did he know what kind of a deal? "We'll work it out. I won't tear down the tree house if you'll promise to stay out of it."

There was a long silence. He could almost see the wheels turning in the kid's head.

"What kind is it—smooth or crunchy?" Dylan asked, his eyes on the sandwiches.

"Smooth," Brandon said.

"Bring it up here," the boy said.

"Nope. You've got to come down," Brandon insisted, keeping his voice calm. He inhaled deeply. "Can't you just smell it now? I can."

"It's not that all-natural kind Mom gets, is it?" he asked.

"Not on your life. I wouldn't have that stuff in my house," Brandon said. "It's full of preservatives and additives." He felt Laura's questioning gaze on him, but he didn't look at her. He kept his eyes on the boy. Pictured him scrambling down the ladder, wolfing down his sandwich and then agreeing to some kind of deal—if not the one he'd mentioned, then one in which Brandon had the tree house removed to some location in town, near their house if the boy agreed not to trespass ever again.

Finally these two would disappear out of his life forever. Then at last—peace and quiet. The solitude he'd been seeking. The only time he'd have to see anybody would be on his terms, when he wanted to. That was the reason he was here. Not for the scenery, not for the horses or the colorful small-town characters. For the right to be alone. *Come on down,* he willed. *Come on.*

"Well...okay."

Brandon heaved a sigh of relief when he heard those words. The next thing he knew the boy was down from his perch and was devouring not only his sandwich, but the other two, as well.

"You got any milk, mister?" Dylan asked, peanut butter smeared across his face.

"Dylan," his mother said sternly, "you can have milk when you get home. You've bothered Mr. Marsh enough for one night."

For one night? He'd been bothered enough for a lifetime.

"If I had it, I'd get it for you, but I don't," Brandon said.

"You're not gonna tear down my tree house?" Dylan asked, his stubborn lower lip jutting out.

Brandon looked up at the tree then down at the boy. "I'll leave it where it is for the moment. If you promise not to come back here unless there's an adult with you. That's the deal. Take it or leave it."

Dylan didn't look happy, but after Laura nudged him a few times he agreed and thanked Brandon for the sandwiches. Brandon nodded and turned to go back to the house. But Laura touched him on the shoulder—such a gentle touch, he thought he might have imagined it.

"Wait," she said. "I have to thank you. I'm sorry for what I said about parenting. I owe you an apology. You obviously have a knack for it that I've lost along the way. This is the second time you've gotten him out of his—I mean your tree—and I'm grateful to you.''

He shrugged off her thanks. ''Just don't let it happen again.''

''It won't. Will it, Dylan?''

This time she had a firm grip on the back of his dirty T-shirt and Dylan had no choice but to agree with her. Brandon wasn't so sure, however. He wanted to ask just how she intended to prevent her son from returning on his own, but not in front of him. Right now he was just grateful the episode was over. Or it would have been over if Dylan hadn't suddenly remembered he really had left his baseball cards there, but they weren't in his room. They were in a cigar box behind the house.

While the boy ran to get them, in the opposite direction from his tree house, Brandon followed Laura to the truck. She got in and lowered the window.

''Were you serious about the deal you made with him?'' she asked.

''Of course. I'm in the business of making deals.''

''With eight-year-olds?'' she asked.

His mouth turned up in a rueful half smile. ''My usual clients are a little older, but a deal is a deal. I said I wouldn't tear it down and I won't. Maybe we need to put it on paper. But not now. We're all tired and hungry. Well, some of us are hungry. I'll be in touch.''

She gave him a quick appraisal with her wide eyes, which made him slightly uncomfortable. He wondered if she interpreted that as a ''Don't call me, I'll call you'' brush-off. That wasn't how he meant it.

She turned on the ignition. He should have kept

his mouth shut, but he couldn't stop the words that came out. He told himself it was her business if her truck was in bad shape. That she wouldn't appreciate hearing what he had to say. But he couldn't resist.

"Don't you hear that grinding sound?" he demanded. It was so loud they could have heard it in the next county.

She tilted her head. "I—I'm not sure."

"How can you not hear it? Don't you know that's your water pump wearing out?"

"It is? Is it serious?" she asked, her eyebrows puckered together.

"Yes, it's serious. It could last a year or it could go out suddenly and you'd lose all your water. The engine would seize up and you'd really be in trouble, stuck on a road somewhere. You need to get a new one."

"How much do they cost?"

"Water pumps? A couple of hundred dollars."

"Then I'll have to take a chance on it lasting a year."

"You can't tell me you don't have enough money for a water pump when you just sold your ranch for the hefty sum I paid for it."

She gave a quick glance over her shoulder toward the house. "This is between you and me, but since you asked, the ranch was mortgaged to the hilt. I'm back to ground zero and living on my salary, which doesn't go very far even here in Silverado," Laura said. "And I'd appreciate it if you'd keep what I've just said to yourself. I'm not looking for sympathy, not from you or from anybody in town."

Brandon nodded slowly. "I can understand that."

"You can?" She gave him a sideways glance out

of the corner of her eye. To her it must look like he had everything. He had an expensive car and he had her ranch. She had no idea that she had the most valuable possession in the world, what he'd give anything for—a son.

There was a long silence. She was waiting, he sensed, for him to elaborate on his statement, but he wasn't ready to do that. He would never be ready to spill his guts to a stranger, to burden someone else with his problems. Instead of waiting here in the driveway, he should just go back to the house. But he didn't do that. Instead he changed the subject. To something else. Something that was on his mind. Would always be on his mind.

"When was the last time you had your brakes relined?"

She blinked. "Uh…"

He shook his head. "Never mind. You don't remember and you can't afford it. Am I right?"

She nodded.

"Is there a decent garage in town?"

"Scotty's," she answered. "But…"

"One of these days when the roads are slick and your brakes fail, you're going to be sorry you didn't pay a visit to Scotty's," he warned.

"Aren't you being a little obsessive, worrying about my truck?" she asked.

He bit back a bitter reply—*Better to be obsessive than dead.* "Well, at least you'll have your cell phone to call for help. No, don't tell me you don't have one."

She shot him a look that would have curdled cream. Before she could follow up with an answer, they both heard Dylan's footsteps. Just in time. The boy got into the car, Dylan and Laura both thanked Brandon and they drove off. At last.

But standing in the driveway, listening to the grinding sound of the water pump and the knocking of the poorly tuned engine, he felt strangely alone. He reminded himself that was what he wanted. To be alone. But this feeling of emptiness was not what he wanted. Back in the house he kept the lights off. The better to ignore the furniture, the rugs and the pictures on the wall that gave evidence of better times, of the family that once lived here. Maybe he'd been wrong to buy somebody else's furnished house.

Damn, he'd forgotten to give her the photograph they'd left. Though it was facedown on the mantel, he could see it in his mind's eye. The picture didn't do her justice. Her hair had a bounce to it that wasn't apparent in the picture. She had a certain spirit that was only hinted at in a photograph. Standing there under the tree, he'd had an irrational desire to touch her hair to see if it would spring back. To see if it felt as silky as it looked.

Her eyes shot sparks in real life, especially when she was angry. Seeing her picture, no one would guess she could exude so much passion—about her son, about her ranch, about everything she cared about. He wondered if she'd cared that much about her husband. The rotten, no-account bastard the Realtor had referred to.

Though he tried not to think about her and her family, it was useless. He couldn't ignore the faint aromas of wood smoke and furniture polish and the roses that climbed the trellis outside the window. In the darkness, those smells became more intense, assaulted his senses and filled him with regret—for what might have been, for himself and for the woman who'd given it all up. He felt sorry for himself and he felt just as sorry for her. He still didn't understand why she'd had to mortgage the place to the hilt, and what went wrong with her marriage. But he sure as hell wasn't going to ask.

Chapter Four

When Laura got back to the bed-and-breakfast, she found the dirty dinner dishes stacked in the sink and her aunt nowhere to be seen. When she investigated, she found her aunt propped up in bed with the night-light on, but still awake.

"That dinner just did me in," Emily explained with an apologetic smile.

"I should have been here to help you," Laura said. Instead of chasing after her unruly son.

"Nonsense," her aunt murmured. "I managed just fine and everyone loved my stuffed cornish game hens. There's one for you and Dylan in the fridge."

"That sounds wonderful. I'm starving, but Dylan just ate three peanut-butter sandwiches, so I imagine he'll pass."

Her aunt smiled understandingly.

Laura got her a drink of water and her pills, and hovered over her aunt's bed, watching her take her medicine. Emily then sent Laura out of the room, saying she was going to sleep. As Laura washed the dishes, though her aunt instructed her sternly to leave them until morning, Dylan drank a tall glass of milk and went to take a shower, another of his most unfavorite things to do.

Laura went upstairs to the charming bedroom she was sharing with her son, the one her aunt had furnished with a hand-painted armoire and original prints of Western scenes done in ochre and tans and browns. She stood at the side of Dylan's bed, studied his flushed face, his damp hair on the pillow, and her heart swelled with love. He was all she had in the world. From now on it was the two of them against the world. If he was being stubborn and troublesome, it was her fault. She was responsible for taking away the underpinnings of his life—his father and his home. What did she expect from him? He was only eight years old, for heaven's sake.

The tree house was a symbol. A symbol of everything he'd lost. She had to find a way to preserve it, to move it to town once she had the housing questions settled. Or build him a new one. She sighed. As if she had the skill or the materials to do that. And even if she did, would Dylan object, saying his dad wouldn't find him there? Whatever kind of a deal Brandon Marsh had made with her son, the bottom line was he eventually wanted the tree house off of his property. And Dylan would never agree to that.

She sighed and bent over to kiss him, a luxury he rarely permitted her, saying he wasn't a baby anymore. She got a whiff of peanut butter on his lips.

Lying in the bed across the room, Laura tossed and turned under the smooth Egyptian cotton sheets her aunt insisted on. She thought about her truck. She wondered if one day she'd be stuck on the highway with a broken water pump. Alone and helpless without a cell phone. She thought about the ranch, not just about the tree house, but about her herb garden, and the main house, wondering where *he* slept, what *he* ate, and why he, a city man with no apparent family, wanted a ranch in the middle of nowhere anyway. Maybe that's what her aunt had learned today, what she'd referred to on the phone.

She shifted from one side to the other. Somewhere a cat yowled and a car horn beeped. No wonder she couldn't sleep. She wasn't in the city, but she sure wasn't in the country anymore. Her thoughts wandered back to the man in her house. If he was a professional negotiator, what was he doing here? Surely his talents were wasted on negotiating a settlement over a tree house.

The next morning she had a chance to talk to Aunt Emily. She deliberately didn't mention Brandon Marsh or the ranch. But her aunt did. A good night's rest seemed to have restored Aunt Emily's strength, and it certainly hadn't dampened her curiosity about the man who'd taken over the McIntyre ranch. As she skillfully rolled out dough for breakfast biscuits for her guests who were still asleep, she eyed Laura who was drinking coffee at the refinished kitchen table and peppered her with questions. Most of them began with why or how.

"As you've noticed, I have a problem with Dylan, Aunt Em," Laura began, glad that Dylan had already bolted down a bowl of cereal and was out on his bike with strict instructions to stay within the city limits, which in the case of Silverado, was about a two-mile square area. "He thinks his father's coming back and that he has to be at the ranch in his tree house to meet up with him. Which is why he went there yesterday. Which is why I called you from the ranch. I was trying to get him to come down out of the tree house.''

''How did you manage that?'' Aunt Emily asked.

''I—uh—I *didn't. He* did it. Brandon, the man who owns the ranch now. He coaxed him down with a peanut-butter sandwich. Three of them to be exact. I don't know why I didn't think of it. Brandon doesn't even like kids. He doesn't want Dylan there. Or me. Or anybody. But somehow he knew what to do.'' She shook her head, still amazed at what had happened.

''Hmmm. Interesting,'' her aunt said.

Laura glanced at her watch. She knew she ought to leave for work. If she got there early she could sort the mail. But her aunt hadn't told her what she'd heard yesterday from Buzz. Laura didn't ask because she didn't want to appear too interested, but after all, the man *was* living on her ranch.

''You say you ran into Buzz yesterday?'' Laura asked finally, unable to contain her curiosity any longer.

''Yes. Everything he told me is confidential, but seeing as the man is living in your house, I think you have a right to know why he's looking for solitude, why he wants his space.''

''Don't tell me it's true he's going to build a theme park or that he's wanted in forty-eight states for bigamy?''

''Or that he's hoping to reopen the silver mine and work it like your great-grandfather did? No, nothing like that. Oh, there's my phone. Let's hope it's a reservation.''

Laura didn't hesitate. That was her cue to leave. No more excuses. She picked up her government-issue blue jacket, waved goodbye to her aunt, who was talking and writing on her calendar, and walked down the street to the post office. She really didn't want to hear Brandon Marsh's story. She wanted to put him out of her mind. Which wasn't easy. She kept picturing him standing in her herb garden soaking wet, his shirt stuck to his chest, his pants stuck to his muscular legs. She kept remembering how it felt to fall into his arms. Twice. No, three times.

What a picture he'd made, this macho man standing there with three peanut-butter sandwiches in his hand, which he'd made himself, coaxing Dylan out of the tree. She reminded herself that his motive was not to help her, but to get rid of them. To do so, he'd had to resort to bribery. And it had worked. What he'd actually do about the tree house remained to be seen.

How could an ordinary woman and an eight-year-old win any concessions from a professional negotiator who held all the cards? Now that he'd gotten Dylan off his land, he'd certainly do everything he could to keep him away. All he'd agreed to was to hold off on the demolition as long as Dylan stayed away. And if he did, she might never hear from him again, and that was for the best. In the cold light of morning, Laura knew that if Brandon really wanted to tear the tree house down, he had every right to. But somehow she knew he'd keep his word with her son. There was something about the look in his eye, the tone of his voice that told her he meant what he said. That he'd make a deal with them. That he was a man of his word. But if he wasn't, she was helpless. All she could do was keep Dylan away from the ranch.

Some days she loved her job. Other days she wondered if this was really where she wanted to spend the next thirty years as the postmistress. That was one of the questions the official from the post office in Reno asked when he'd interviewed her yesterday.

"How long do you plan to stay with the Post Office? We're looking for stability," the man had said. "Your predecessor has provided the community with continuous service."

"I know. Willa Mae is my role model. I only hope I can live up to her reputation," Laura had replied sincerely. "My only desire is to serve the community." Well, that wasn't her *only* desire. She also desired to make enough money to support herself and her son, and to look forward to a government pension in thirty years so she could retire. No, she didn't plan to move to Reno and kick up her heels the way Willa Mae did.

Laura pictured herself in a small house in town where she'd sit in her rocker and watch the action from her front porch in her twilight years. If she was lucky enough to get this job. If she was lucky enough to have twilight years. "Is anyone else applying for the job?" she'd asked. Even if she didn't have the highest grade on the qualifying exam, she might get the job by default.

"I can't tell you that," he'd said stiffly and wound up the interview by saying she'd know in two weeks if she had the job.

What would she do if she didn't get the job? Silverado was not exactly a hotbed of activity and employment opportunities. Where would they live if she didn't get Willa Mae's apartment over the post office? They couldn't stay at the bed-and-breakfast forever. The minute Aunt Emily had to turn down a paying guest because she and Dylan were occupying a room, Laura would feel so guilty she'd have to leave. No matter how kind her aunt was, she had a business to run, not a shelter for poor relatives.

BRANDON PACED back and forth on the deck of the ranch house waiting for a call from a client. It was quiet out there. Too quiet. Yes, that was what he wanted. Yes, that was the reason he'd moved there. But for the past week he'd been restless. He told himself it was just a matter of adjusting to his new life. It would take a while. He'd expected the boy to come back to the tree house. But he hadn't. He wasn't disappointed. He was relieved.

He'd gone to town yesterday to pick up a week's worth of mail, but it was lunchtime and a different young woman was behind the counter. He was relieved to see Laura wasn't there. He wouldn't have known what to say to her if he had seen her. He was just relieved that Dylan hadn't returned to the ranch. A deal is only a good deal if both parties feel satisfied. In this case, Brandon did, but he was sure the boy didn't. Not if it kept him away from his beloved tree house.

In many circles Brandon was known for his skill in doing just that—making everybody involved in a negotiation somewhat happy, with both parties feeling like they'd come out on top. But he'd never been personally involved before. After picking up his mail he drove back toward the ranch, feeling oddly let down. And spent the rest of the day sitting on the wide veranda staring off at the hills in the distance.

He'd once thought that doing his work on the

ranch would be no problem. Thanks to his computer, his modem and his fax machine, most of his work these days could be done anywhere. So he'd thought. But he was having trouble concentrating these days. His mind still drifted back to the past and to the tragedy that had changed his life forever. But sometimes, without his knowing how or why, he thought about the family who lived in this house, imagining how life was for them before events had forced them to move away. From his perspective, that hardly counted as a tragedy, but for them, he imagined it did.

Some days like today, he found himself in a kind of limbo, not living in the past, but not really connected to the present, either. He thought of himself as straddling a rough-hewn wooden fence like the one that bordered the ranch, where one good push could land him squarely in the past or in the future. So after checking his messages and sending a couple of faxes and finally getting a call from the client, he didn't know what to do with himself. He decided to take his car out for a test run. He'd told Dylan his car could go one hundred and twenty—that's what it said in a popular car magazine—but he hadn't actually tested it.

One thing about Nevada—there was little traffic on the long stretch of black macadam, and few speed limits were observed. For someone with a high-performance car, these roads were a definite draw. For someone who'd loved cars since he was a kid, who'd read car magazines as a teenager and dreamed of owning a car like this, Nevada was a driver's paradise. Yes, it was a definite temptation to let the car go.

He put the top down and felt the hot wind sting his face. He watched the speedometer needle climb and his spirits rose along with it. One hundred, one-ten... But the steering was heavy, not the response he expected from his car at this speed. He slowed down, and the steering got worse. There was a growling sound when he turned the steering wheel. What the hell was going on here?

He pulled off the road onto a soft shoulder and checked under the hood. The power steering reservoir was bone-dry! Thank God he caught it. If he'd driven any farther he might have ruined the power steering pump. But now what? Who did he call? Did they even have a tow truck in Silverado?

He had his cell phone but he didn't know who to call.

What was the name of the garage Laura had mentioned? Scotty's—yes that was it. He called Information, got the number and Scotty promised to send a tow truck for him. The kid who came said he was Scotty's son. He didn't look a day over sixteen. He took a moment to stand on the side of the road and admire the sleek lines, the smooth finish and the hood ornament of Brandon's car.

"Nice car," he said respectfully.

"Thanks."

"How fast can she do?"

"One hundred twenty."

Impressed, he whistled. Then he got down to business and looked under the hood. "Looks like you need a new power steering hose."

Brandon nodded. "I don't suppose you have one in stock."

The kid shrugged. "You'll have to ask my dad."

Brandon rode in the cab of the truck with his eye on his car in the rearview mirror.

"This is the first time my dad's let me drive the tow truck," the boy said proudly.

"Really?" Brandon kept his eyes glued to his car behind them, his confidence only slightly shaken by this statement.

"Yep. The garage is so busy today my dad couldn't spare anyone else. Anyone with experience," the boy confessed cheerfully.

"He must have confidence in you," Brandon noted.

"Guess so. He's taught me everything he knows. I've been working for him after school and during vacations since I could reach the steering wheel of a car. After high school my dad's gonna make me an apprentice and pay me union wage."

"Then you're going to stay right here in Silverado?" Brandon asked. He would have thought most high school kids would be on the first bus out of town after graduation, looking for jobs and excitement. But this kid said he had no desire to leave Silverado. Why should he? He thought it was the best place for a kid to grow up. Brandon knew it was rare for a teenager to respect his father the way this kid obviously did, and he wondered how it happened. Maybe it was easier in a small town. He didn't know. Even more important was that the father obviously respected the kid, or he wouldn't let him drive the tow truck, would he?

Scotty's was located just off Main Street. The lot was full of cars with two or three mechanics working on them. Scotty himself was tall and solid and seemed to be everywhere at once. Brandon had to wait a half hour before Scotty wiped his hands on a clean rag and inspected Brandon's car.

"Your son tells me I'm going to need a new power steering hose," Brandon said.

Scotty smiled proudly. "Smart boy. He's right. Yes, this one's sprung a leak. Never know when that's going to happen or where. I don't have any in stock. We don't get many of these cars. But I can order you one from Reno."

"How long will that take?" Brandon asked.

"If they have it in stock, I might have it for you tomorrow," Scotty said.

"Tomorrow?" *Might* have it for you tomorrow? How was he going to get back to the ranch? How was he going to get back here tomorrow? How was he going to get along without his car?

"Give me a call first, before you come in," Scotty said.

"You the guy who bought the McIntyre place?"

"Yes."

"Nice piece of land. Last of the big spreads. What are you going to do with it?" Scotty asked.

"Live there," Brandon said.

Scotty gave him a swift appraisal. "By yourself?" he asked.

Brandon was tempted to tell him he was going to turn it into a Wild West brothel. Why not start another rumor in a town that fed on them like cattle fed on hay? But he just nodded and asked Scotty to remove the scratch in the fender while he was at it.

"By the way, you reline brakes, right?" Brandon asked.

"Sure."

"And replace water pumps?"

"Of course."

"Just wondered," Brandon said.

He walked away from the garage feeling what might be called separation anxiety in some circles. To be without his car was unthinkable. If this was San Francisco, it wouldn't take that long to get a part. If this was San Francisco, he'd rent a car. If this was San Francisco... But it wasn't. This was Silverado. If he didn't know it before, he knew it now. So much for isolation and small-town charm.

He was stuck in the middle of town with nothing to do but walk aimlessly down Main Street and think about Laura driving a beat-up old truck. She didn't believe him when he told her how dangerous it was. She thought he was some kind of obsessive nut. Maybe he was, but if he could prevent another accident, it was worth it.

This was not the kind of town where you called a cab. This was the kind of town where you called a relative or a friend. He only had one friend and he wasn't sure she'd consider herself one. And if he did call her, what would she say? Would she feel obliged to point out the irony of his worries about her old truck when it was his expensive new car that had failed on the highway?

He walked by the hardware store with its display of tools and heavy equipment, the drugstore and the feed-and-fuel store, and he realized there were no boutiques, no souvenir shops or galleries. Everything for sale was something needed for everyday life. Every building was utilitarian except for the beautiful large restored Victorian house on the corner with the sign on a plaque that announced it was the Silverado Historical Society.

Brandon stood for a moment studying the gingerbread trim and the stained-glass window above the door, thinking about the gold and silver rush that made it all possible. Picturing Laura's great-grandfather turning over a greenish mass and finding silver. Then he turned around and cut through the grassy town square with its turreted bandstand that looked as if it had been there for at least one hundred years and headed for the post office. Through the window he saw Laura behind the counter. She was leaning forward, talking earnestly to a customer.

He thought she was probably good at her job; she seemed to like helping people. He remembered how she'd offered to show him around on the first day he'd arrived. How he'd brusquely turned her down. He tried to imagine why Dylan's father had left them. A woman like that, with her looks, and intelligence, her drive and determination, the way she stood up for her son. The guy had to be crazy. She'd find someone else. But who?

Suddenly she looked up and he caught her eye. Laura's face paled, then her cheeks turned red. She hadn't expected to see Brandon Marsh, though it shouldn't have come as a complete surprise since he had to come in to pick up his mail if he wanted it. But he hadn't been in all week, at least not when she was there. In any case, there was no reason to react this way. With alternating chills and fever as if she had the flu. She'd been trying to help Madge Silverstone find her daughter's zip code, but now the numbers swam in front of her eyes.

Finally Madge turned around to follow Laura's gaze, to see what the distraction was. "Who's that?" she asked, peering over her bifocals.

"Brandon Marsh, the man who bought my ranch," Laura said.

"Good looking son of a gun," the old lady said with a chuckle. "What's he staring at you for?"

"I...ah..." Laura wanted to deny he was staring at her, but she couldn't. He *was* staring. And his penetrating gaze made it impossible for her to look away. With his tall, rangy frame, broad shoulders and rugged features, he was without a doubt the best-looking man to set foot in Silverado for a long time. Maybe ever. Which was no excuse to stare back at him.

"Probably waiting for me to clear out so he can pick up his mail," Madge said, turning back to the zip code directory. "I hear he's quite a loner."

"Really. Where did you hear that?"

"Oh, I forget. Somebody who heard it from Buzz."

Buzz the Realtor. She should have known. And Brandon should have known better than to tell Buzz anything. But he didn't. He knew nothing about small towns and the way gossip spread. Well, he'd learn.

As if he'd heard them discussing him, Brandon was gone when she looked up. She wanted to run out on the street and ask him where he was going. To tell him to come back and get his mail. But of course she didn't. That would be highly unprofessional. And unnecessary. If he didn't want his mail, he could leave it in his box. It was no business of hers. After Madge left, Laura refused to stand staring out the window waiting and watching. Instead she sorted outgoing boxes for the late afternoon pickup.

A while later he was back. Without a greeting, as

if she was no more than a government employee there to serve him and the rest of the public he asked for his mail. When she handed him a packet of magazines and envelopes, her hand brushed his. His gaze met hers. Did he feel something? Anything? Did he feel the same electric shock she did? Was his skin covered with goose bumps like hers was? Of course not. If it was, he'd never let on.

There was no one else in the post office. The mail lay forgotten on the counter. The silence stretched between them. She looked at the clock and watched the seconds tick by as she tried to think of something to say. She wanted to ask where he'd been all week, she wanted to hear how pleased he was that Dylan hadn't violated their agreement, but he didn't speak.

Finally he broke the silence. "I have a problem," he said. "With my car. I don't want to bother you, but I don't know anyone else and I need help."

"Help with your car?" She gasped in surprise. So that's why he stood there without speaking. He was reluctant to ask her for help. "I'm not the one to ask. I don't know anything about cars, as you well know."

"You don't have to. All I need is a ride home. My car's at Scotty's Garage. My power steering hose sprung a leak and they have to order a new one. It won't be ready for at least another day," he said.

She stifled a smile.

"I know what you're thinking," he said. "Go ahead and gloat. Because your beat-up truck is still running, while my new car, for all the work and money I've put into it, is in the garage."

"I didn't say a word," she protested.

''But you're thinking it. You're thinking how ironic it is.''

Yes, that was exactly what she was thinking. Not that she'd ever admit it. Because he didn't look like he was in the mood for irony. He looked annoyed that anything could go wrong with his car. Not only that, he looked like she was the last person he wanted to ask for help. But he had no choice.

''I'm not thinking anything of the sort,'' she protested. ''You don't know what I'm thinking unless you're telepathic. And if you were, you'd know that's not what I'm thinking. And I don't gloat. Now what can I do for you?'' she asked, crossing her arms over her waist.

''You could give me a ride home, if you don't mind. I'd call a taxi, but...''

''There are no taxis in Silverado,'' she said. ''I'd be glad to give you a ride. But as you can see, I'm all alone here, so you'll have to wait until five when I get off. Another thing. You'll have to ride in my truck. The brakes could go out or the water pump could fail anytime.'' She was aware that if she wasn't gloating, she was being sarcastic. It did give her some satisfaction to stick it to him, however gently, after the way he'd come down on her for failing to maintain her truck. ''We'd be stuck,'' she added. ''Because *I* don't have a cell phone.''

He pulled his phone from his shirt pocket. ''But I do.'' He looked at his watch. What did he think, that she'd drop everything and drive him home now?

''There's the coffee shop,'' she suggested.

''Don't worry about me. I have plenty to do.''

''Then you can meet me at my aunt's a little after

five. It's the big lavender Victorian on Spring Street just off the town square."

"Thank you. I appreciate this."

"Don't mention it," she said.

Brandon went to the coffee shop. When he said he had plenty to do, he was lying. He had nothing to do but wait for her. It was only three-thirty. She may have had plans for after work, but she'd graciously said yes anyway. What if she had a date? After all, she was divorced or separated, wasn't she? She'd told him that Dylan's father was not coming back. She was free to go out. He wondered for the second time that day whom she'd date in this town.

Sitting at the counter in the café he observed the other customers. Most were men who looked like ranchers. If she was in the market for another rancher, this was the place to look. *If* she was in the market... And she should be. How was she going to support herself on the salary of a postmistress? Living in town in a rented house after having a ranch would be quite a comedown. Not that she'd ever admit it. She was too proud. He was surprised she'd admitted she didn't have enough money for car repairs.

"You the new fella out at the McIntyre ranch?" the waitress asked, handing him a menu.

"How did you know?" he asked. Would he ever get used to small-town curiosity? Or the fact that everyone knew everything about everybody else? Or wouldn't rest until they did? He was just grateful no one knew all about him. Or did they? No, if they did, they'd get that familiar pitying look in their eyes, and they'd tiptoe around him, afraid to talk about death or accidents or children. At least Laura McIntyre didn't know. She was as transparent as the glass window with U.S. Post Office written in gold-edged letters across it. If she did know, he'd see it in her eyes, hear it in the tone of her voice. Her anguish over her son, her regret at leaving the ranch, her shame at not having enough money to pay for car repairs were all blatantly evident by the expressions on her face. She'd make a terrible poker player.

"We don't get that many strangers," the waitress said. "How do you like it out there?"

"Fine," he said.

"Too bad about Laura. Never thought she'd ever sell the ranch."

"You're a friend of hers?" he asked.

"We were in high school together," she said. "She was prom queen, class president, honor society. Could have been anything. But all she wanted was to stay here, get married and have kids. But then..."

"How's the pie?" Brandon asked. He was sure Laura would not want her friend to be recounting her life story to a stranger in the café. He certainly didn't want to hear her story from anyone, least of all the waitress.

"Just come out of the oven," she said. "Can I get you a piece with some coffee?"

He nodded, and when she returned with his order she tilted her head to one side to observe him more closely. "What's your deal?" she asked. "You gonna run cattle?"

"No, no cattle."

"Raise horses?"

"I don't think so."

"Grow wheat, oats, barley?"

"No."

"What then?"

"I'm just going to enjoy the view." And the solitude. He was beginning to regret ever coming into the café. He had no idea that he as a stranger was fair game.

"By yourself?" she asked incredulously.

"That's right," he said firmly and poured cream into his coffee.

"Gonna join the Grange?"

"I'm not sure." He didn't know what the Grange was, but didn't want to join it or anything else, whatever it was.

"All the ranchers belong. Laura's great-grandfather started it. She belongs. Everyone does."

"Oh," he said, picked up his fork and took a bite of warm cherry pie. "Then I guess I'll have to join," he said. Anything to get her off his case.

"What about the historical society?"

"I just got here," Brandon said. "I don't know anything about the history."

"Good way to learn. They've got lectures and pamphlets, meetings every month," she said.

"Uh-huh. I'll think about it."

"Well," the waitress said apologetically, "I gotta go now. Enjoy."

He did enjoy the pie. Then somehow he managed to kill enough time by walking aimlessly from one end of town to the other, then buying the local newspaper and reading it on a bench in the town square. Just when he hoped he'd blended into the scenery behind his newspaper, someone stopped, sat down and advised him to subscribe to the *Silverado Bulletin.*

"It's cheaper that way," the man said. "And you get it delivered to your door."

"Not my door. Nothing gets delivered to my door," Brandon said, lowering his paper to regard the older man with the mustache sitting next to him. "Not yet, anyway. But I'm working on it. Are you in charge of circulation?"

"David Ray, editor-in-chief," he said, and shook Brandon's hand. "You must be the man—"

"Who bought the McIntyre ranch. Brandon Marsh."

They shook hands and talked about the town, the McIntyres and the newspaper, or rather, David talked and Brandon listened. David asked Brandon what kind of business he was in. He told Brandon he'd like to do a feature story on him, and Brandon told David he'd rather he didn't. He preferred anonymity. David told Brandon he shouldn't miss the Fourth of July parade and picnic sponsored by the newspaper. Just to be polite, Brandon said he'd be there. But he wouldn't.

It was on the Fourth of July two years ago when his wife and child were killed. Even if it was an ordinary day, those kind of holidays were for families, and Brandon had no desire to watch kids eating hot dogs and fathers playing baseball. He asked directions to the bed-and-breakfast.

"If you get an invitation to dinner there, don't turn it down," David advised. "She's the best cook in town. Not bad to look at, either." A wistful note crept into the man's voice. Brandon made a hasty departure before David got started on another story about the McIntyres or the town. Not that they weren't interesting; they were. But he didn't want to get involved. He just wanted to get his car fixed and retire to the ranch once and for all. Except for his trips to the post office, he didn't want to meet any more townsfolk.

He didn't want to make new friends and he didn't want to see his old friends. And he didn't want to have to come to town to get his mail. He reminded himself to make a call to somebody he knew in Washington who knew someone at the central post office. Having no delivery service was something for the historical society, not present-day Silverado.

"Yes?" The woman who opened the door to the large, frame house with the turrets and gables and spacious front porch, eyed him with undisguised curiosity. Which he'd come to expect from the inhabitants of Silverado. Might as well be up-front. It would save a lot of questions in the long run.

"I'm Brandon Marsh, the man who bought the Silver Springs Ranch and I'm looking for Laura." He had half a mind to add, just in case she was as interested as other people he'd met, that he was single, living there alone and he liked it that way. That he had no intention of doing anything with the ranch but live there and that he didn't want to hear anything about Laura or her ex-husband. But he didn't say that. This, after all, might very well be the aunt he'd heard about. The one who was such a great cook and "not bad to look at, either." Yes, the description fit. She was at least fifty, but her face was unlined and her figure trim. So all he said was "She told me to meet her here."

The woman smiled. "I'm Emily Eckhart, Laura's aunt. She isn't back from work yet. Come in and wait inside. You must be Laura's date."

He frowned. "No. I didn't know she had a date. In that case, I won't impose on her. Thanks anyway." Laura could have told him she had a date. He turned to go, but she stopped him.

"Wait," she said. Now it was her turn to return his puzzled frown. "What I meant was...I thought you were... Silly me, I thought you were her date. Oh, never mind. Won't you have a glass of sherry?" She led him into the formal living room and poured him a glass of amber liquid from a decanter on the coffee table, though he'd never said he wanted a drink. When she handed it to him, she looked him up and down. He wondered if her niece had mentioned him to her. He wondered if she might have said that he was a loner and a fanatic about car safety.

Before Laura's aunt could barrage him with the usual questions, he took the opportunity to comment on the charming decor and the wonderful smell coming from the kitchen. And it worked.

She beamed. "It's veal chops in wild mushroom sauce. Do you object to eating meat? No? Well, then I hope you'll join us tonight. I know it's not fashionable to serve veal these days or rich sauces, but what can I say, I'm an old-fashioned girl. And my guests don't complain."

"I would think not. I understand you're an outstanding cook," Brandon said.

"Now where did you hear that?" Emily asked with a coy smile.

"Just now, out on the street. A man named David mentioned it."

"David, David Ray?" He might have been mistaken, but he could have sworn the woman blushed. "That devil. What else did he say?"

"He advised me not to miss the Fourth of July celebration," Brandon said.

"Quite right. If you've never been to a small town on the Fourth—"

Brandon admitted he hadn't.

"Then you're in for a treat. Some might call it corny, but to me it's the essence of what America stands for. Well, Laura should be along any minute now. She's a wonderful cook herself. Just the other day she made a berry cobbler for me. Delicious, just delicious."

The bell on the oven timer rang, and before Brandon could tell her he couldn't possibly stay for dinner, no matter how many townfolk raved about her cooking, Aunt Emily excused herself to go to the kitchen. "That will be my chocolate cake," she explained. "Just make yourself at home."

Brandon walked around the room, sipping the excellent Spanish sherry and looking at pictures on the wall. And wondering where Laura was. In his experience, post offices opened and closed promptly. But this was not San Francisco, as Laura had so succinctly pointed out. This was Silverado. He'd better get used to it.

Chapter Five

He finally saw her coming down the street, walking briskly, her arms swinging at her sides. Was she in a hurry to see him? Hardly. But just for a split second he wished she was. He reminded himself that if she was in a hurry, it was to get rid of him. He stood at the window and watched her. He had no idea anyone could look that good in a post office uniform, but she did. It fit her like it was made for her. Her hair brushed the collar of her white blouse and the skirt hugged her hips. Absently he wondered how she'd look in something else. Something loose, something soft. Something silky like her skin.

He caught himself before his traitorous thoughts ran away with him. He didn't know what was wrong with him. How could he let a woman get under his skin this way? Someone he hardly knew. Someone with such a different background from his. He walked out the front door to meet her on the sidewalk, hoping they'd jump in her truck and be on their way. And then he'd never waste another fruitless afternoon in town again once he got his car. And he'd never wonder about Laura or worry about her truck or her son again.

"I'm sorry I'm late," she said breathlessly, her cheeks flushed. "Charlie Rogers dropped his bank book in the mailbox in front of the post office. I had to unlock the box and we had to go through all the mail to find it."

He shook his head. "Service above and beyond the call of duty. Don't give it a thought. Your aunt was good enough to give me a glass of sherry." He was still holding his glass and couldn't help noticing her eyes were the same amber color.

"She's always the perfect hostess. I'll just be a minute, then we can go. Dylan's at a friend's house, but I have to tell my aunt where I'm going, unless you did."

"I didn't have a chance," he said and gritted his teeth. Another delay.

"She talks a lot," she admitted. Laura was gone longer than a minute, and when she came back she'd changed into a denim skirt and a T-shirt. As if he'd read her thoughts. It was a buttery soft T-shirt that outlined her small, rounded breasts.

He jerked his gaze away and wondered why in the hell she had to change when she knew he was in a hurry. When she knew he'd just spent all afternoon cooling his heels wandering around town talking to strangers. And if she had to change, why couldn't she have changed into a shapeless tent of a dress? Did she have to wear something so provocative? He clenched his hands into fists as his heart pounded. He had to get out of there.

"My aunt says you're staying to dinner," she said. Her forehead was creased. She didn't look pleased.

"Oh, no. She invited me, but I can't stay. Please

tell her I couldn't impose. And I've got to be getting back.''

''It's too late. She's already set the table. You'll hurt her feelings if you don't stay,'' she said bluntly.

''Are you sure?'' he asked. He had to get out of this. He couldn't spend another minute in this sexy woman's company. She didn't even know she was sexy. That was the problem. One of the problems. His mind raced for possible solutions. Maybe he could even borrow Dylan's bike and pedal back to the ranch. But she was right. It was too late. He exhaled loudly and gave in to the inevitable.

It wasn't as bad as he thought it would be. David was right. The dinner was excellent. The other guests who were staying the night in one of Emily's guest rooms were a couple from Arizona who were under the mistaken impression that he and Laura were a couple, maybe because her aunt had seated them together. At least that way he didn't have to look at her across the white linen tablecloth. To listen to her talk and watch her smile politely and force himself to look elsewhere than at her face under candlelight.

He did notice that Laura kept looking at her watch during dinner, and he didn't blame her. She didn't want him there any more than he wanted to be there. He was a constant reminder of what she'd lost. Just as she and her son were the same to him. Yes, she was just as anxious as he was for him to leave. Besides, he wasn't very good company. That's what his friends said as they urged him to lighten up, to move on with his life and find someone new. As if Jeanne could be replaced. As if another child could replace his son.

Tonight he made an effort. He answered questions

and he even asked them. He found Laura's aunt to be a fount of information on the history of the town and the part the McIntyres played in it. She gave a pitch for the historical society, telling Brandon he was entitled to join, now that he owned a historical piece of property.

"Many people made a quick fortune here in Silverado," her aunt said. "And just as quickly lost it. The town needs new blood and so does our historical society."

He couldn't help notice how quiet Laura was and how she seemed to take those last remarks personally. She set her fork down and from then on she scarcely said a word. As soon as it was possible, she excused herself and him, saying she had to give him a ride home.

"So you live here, lucky girl," said one of the guests to Laura.

"Temporarily," she said.

"And you live on a ranch," said the other to Brandon. "By yourself."

"That's right," he said firmly, and thanked Laura's aunt for the dinner before they went out to her truck.

"There's just one thing," Laura said as she backed her truck out of her aunt's driveway. "You can't say a word about this truck or I swear I'll dump you out somewhere along the highway."

"I won't. Look, I'm sorry if I offended you. I was trying to be helpful, that's all. But you've got the last laugh. You're the one who's rescued me. Tell me, does it every bother you that everyone in town knows everything about you?"

"Everything? I hope they don't know everything.'' But in her heart she knew they probably did know almost everything. ''Yes, of course it bothers me. I hate it. I was going to warn you not to talk too much. Not to tell anyone anything you don't want the whole town to know. But you've already figured that out.'' Of course he had. He was smart enough to keep his private life private. Except for what he'd told Buzz. And that was before he'd moved here, before he'd realized what a small town was all about.

They drove in the dark to the ranch. It was a warm, moonless night. Cicadas buzzed in the fields along the road. Laura didn't know what more to say so she didn't say anything. Neither did he. She knew that it must have cost Brandon a lot of pride to ask her for a favor. When she pulled into the driveway at the ranch he got out and thanked her.

''Give me a call when they get your car fixed, and I'll come and pick you up. Before or after work, that is,'' she said.

''Thank you,'' he said. ''Oh, wait a minute. You left a picture on the mantel. I'll get it for you.''

''That's all right,'' she said, but he was already in the house. She considered pulling away. She didn't want the picture. She didn't want to wait for him. She didn't want to wait in her own driveway and realize it wasn't hers anymore. The idea that she'd lost the house and the ranch because of her own stupidity, by making the wrong choice of a husband, caused a pain in her chest. The farther away from the ranch, the less it hurt. But she couldn't just take off now. It would be rude. She got out of the truck to stretch her legs and to inhale the fragrance of the jasmine bushes that lined the driveway, the ones her grandmother had planted so many years ago.

"Here," he said, appearing out of the dark and handing her the picture.

She knew just what picture it was. She didn't want it. Maybe that's why she "inadvertently" left it behind. It was a reminder of happier times and her biggest mistake. "You should have just thrown it away," she said, placing it in the back of the truck. Her voice wavered despite her determination to be strong. To look ahead instead of back. "I meant to, but I didn't."

"Was it that bad?" he asked gravely, putting his hands on her shoulders.

"No, of course not," she said, knowing instantly that he meant the marriage and not the picture. She felt the warmth of his hands and had the most overwhelming desire to lean against him, to draw on his strength, to find comfort from a stranger. What was wrong with her? She who'd refused to rely on anyone after the divorce. She'd kept everything bottled up inside herself for years. It must be the warm summer night, the unexpected touch of a man's hands. The unexpected sympathy in his voice. But she couldn't let herself do that. She couldn't depend on anyone ever again. She'd learned her lesson. At least she hoped she had.

She'd never admit to anyone how she'd suffered through the last few years, watching the ranch slide downhill, helpless to stop it. "There were good times," she assured him. If only she could remember them. Focus on them. "What hurts is that it was all my fault."

"What do you mean?" he asked.

"I made a bad decision," she said, as the words tumbled out. "To marry someone I didn't really know. I could have married someone from here. Someone I'd known all my life. Someone from a ranching family, but no, that would have been too easy, too dull. I was looking for excitement. He came breezing into town and suddenly I was—'' She broke off, embarrassed to be doing exactly what she'd told him not to. Confiding her troubles in a stranger. Telling tales she certainly wouldn't want the whole town to know.

''Swept off your feet?'' he suggested.

''Yes, exactly. I should have known. I should have listened to my parents. Somehow they knew it wouldn't work out. That he'd run through my money, cause me to lose everything with one of his schemes, raising thoroughbreds or turning grain into ethanol or—'' She broke off, unable to continue.

The enormity of what she'd done, ignoring her parents' advice, losing the ranch they'd spent a lifetime building up welled up inside her and she couldn't stop the tears. She hadn't cried when Jason left, she hadn't cried when she'd signed the deed to the ranch, but somehow, tonight in the company of the last man in the world who would understand her, who would care about her, she burst into helpless tears.

''Laura,'' he said, alarmed. ''Are you all right?'' She looked up into his eyes, and the concern she saw there made her cry even harder. More than concern, it was understanding. She let go with great, gulping sobs. Why, when she didn't know him and he didn't know her would she let down barriers she'd kept in place for months? The tears streamed down her face. ''I—I'm sorry, I can't—''

"Go ahead," he said, putting his arms around her and holding her tight. "Let go. Cry it out."

She wrapped her arms around his neck, pressed her face against his chest and drenched his shirt with her tears.

"It's okay," he said roughly.

She knew it wasn't okay. It wasn't okay to fall apart like this. But she couldn't stop crying. It felt so good to let go for a change. To stop acting brave and tough when she was dying inside. To have someone to lean on, someone to make soothing sounds in her ear, someone to hold her.

When her tears had been reduced to mere sniffles, he brushed a tear from her cheek with the back of his thumb. The unexpected gentleness of his touch made her knees weak. If he let go of her now she'd fall down in a heap in the driveway. But he didn't. Instead, he kissed her.

The shock of his kiss hit her like a flash flood in the Nevada desert. Out of the blue and completely unexpected. But was it so unexpected? Or unwanted? Hadn't she been thinking about this man since he first accosted her on this same driveway? If she were honest, wouldn't she have to admit that he'd fascinated her, annoyed her and attracted her with his mysterious past, his granite jaw and his unfathomable dark eyes?

Whatever she'd thought, she was no longer thinking anymore. She was only feeling. At first it was only a brush of his lips across hers, tasting, testing, experimenting, trying… It wasn't enough. Not for her. Not for him. He kissed her then with a pent-up passion she sensed he'd been holding back for a long time. A long time before she'd met him. She didn't know. She didn't care. All she cared about was him and her and now. She was no longer someone's mother, someone's ex-wife, someone's daughter and someone else's niece. She was just a woman. A woman who needed a man. This man. Now.

With his arms around her waist, he pulled her close, closer and deepened the kiss. His tongue slid between her lips and came deep and slow into her mouth. The heat that coiled in her body made her feel she might burst into flames. She'd never felt like this. Never. Not even with Jason. Not even when he'd swept her off her feet.

She clung to Brandon, returned his kisses, letting herself get swept along on a tide of passion she didn't know existed. Until the phone in his back pocket rang. He reached for it. She pulled away. She stared, dazed while he answered the phone. His voice was hoarse and he was breathing hard. But not as hard as she was.

She didn't know who it was. She didn't know what he said. She only knew she'd gone a little crazy and lost her head. The ringing of the phone had restored her senses. And his. Thank heavens. Without hesitating she jumped in her truck and left the ranch in a cloud of dust. Not that he noticed or cared. He was on the phone. He'd let a phone call come between them. That was all it meant to him. If the phone hadn't rung, where would they be? What would they be doing?

Her imagination went wild picturing various scenarios as she drove. The two of them in her house, on the floor or on the couch. Him carrying her up the stairs. Making love to her in her old bed, on her sheets. The summer breeze wafting in the window, cooling her feverish skin. Their passion going out of control. And all of the time a voice inside her head was saying she had to stop. It was wrong. None of these visions contributed to her driving safely. All of them made her hands shake on the steering wheel and her face flame.

Shame suffused her body. He must be wondering what kind of a wanton woman would let him kiss her like that? And what was worse, kissing him back? Hadn't she learned her lesson nine years ago when another handsome stranger came to town? Was she so starved for affection she couldn't keep her hands off the man? Affection? That wasn't affection; that was passion. She knew the difference.

She found her son on the front porch with his friend Brian trading baseball cards. He was so engrossed he barely noticed her. Even if he had, he wouldn't have noticed her hair was a mess and her cheeks were tearstained. He was an eight-year-old, after all. Her aunt was another matter. Laura stopped in the powder room, splashed water on her face and combed her hair. Then she went to the kitchen.

Her aunt turned from the sink where she was washing dishes, dried her hands on her apron and surveyed her niece. Laura blushed under her scrutiny, sure she could tell what had happened between Laura and Brandon.

''You've been holding out on me,'' her aunt said, her mouth curved in a half smile.

''What do you mean?'' Laura said. Could her aunt possibly know what she'd been doing?

''He's a charming man.''

Charming? He was good-looking, he was stubborn, he was rich and he was smart. And, oh, yes, he was sexy. But charming?

"Yes," her aunt continued. "Too charming to be buried by himself out there at the ranch. After what he's been through."

"I think he likes it out there," Laura said mildly, ignoring the part about "what he's been through." If Brandon wanted her to know what he'd been through, he'd tell her. Right now, she didn't want to know any more about him. She wanted to forget about him, forget what happened tonight. If she could. She'd made a fool of herself, crying and throwing herself at him.

"That doesn't mean he doesn't need some stimulating company from time to time."

"You don't mean me," Laura protested.

"I certainly do."

"You're the one who's stimulating," Laura said. "That's why you're such a good hostess."

"Why, thank you, Laura. I never did get a chance to tell you what I learned about Brandon Marsh, did I?"

"No, but..." What could she say? "It's none of my business." That would hurt her aunt's feelings. She picked up a dish towel and rubbed a wineglass dry until it sparkled. Waiting, half dreading what she was about to hear.

"Well, he's a consultant," her aunt said. "And very successful. He's going to do all his work on the ranch. He doesn't need to see his clients. He can do all his business by phone and computers. What do you think of that?" she asked.

Laura breathed a sigh of relief mixed with disappointment. Maybe she did want to know more about him after all. Maybe she wanted to know if he'd ever been married. If her aunt knew, she wasn't saying.

"That's all?" Laura asked.

"Yes. What did you expect?"

"Nothing," she said.

Her aunt washed and she dried. They talked about everything but Brandon, then she went out to find Dylan and sent him to bed.

When the phone rang an hour later, she was lying in bed reading, or trying to read when her mind was anywhere but on the article about single parents raising successful children.

Laura sat up straight in bed and glanced at Dylan, who was tangled in his sheets, but sound asleep. Then she tiptoed to the door and heard her aunt say, "Just a moment. I'll check."

Standing there in her cotton nightshirt, Laura shivered. Somehow she knew the call was for her and she knew who it was. She could have slipped back into the room, buried herself under the covers and pretended to be asleep. That would have been the prudent thing to do, because she didn't want to talk to whoever it was on the phone. Didn't want to have to apologize for her behavior, didn't want to even acknowledge it. It might have been the prudent thing to do, but it was also the cowardly thing to do. And she knew that sooner or later she'd have to face Brandon and put this unfortunate incident behind them.

She tiptoed down the stairs just as her aunt was coming to look for her.

"Oh, there you are. It's for you. I thought you'd gone to bed," she said in a half whisper. "Everyone else has."

"Thanks." Laura took the cordless phone and as her aunt went down the hall to her bedroom, she waved, a little smile playing on her lips before she closed her bedroom door behind her.

"Yes?" Laura said, sinking into the deep sofa in front of the fireplace. The only light came from the antique gas lamps flanking the fireplace.

"Look," Brandon said, "I'm sorry to be calling so late, but I had to apologize for what happened. I'm sorry."

Her heart sank. She should have known he'd regret the kiss. "So am I," she said quickly. What else could she say? She was ashamed of how she'd behaved, but sorry? She wasn't sorry it happened. There was a long silence. She didn't know what else to say. Was that it? Was she supposed to hang up?

"I wouldn't be honest if I said I was sorry about the kiss. That's not it. I'm only sorry the phone rang when it did. I should have ignored it, but from force of habit, I didn't. I wanted to tell you that I haven't kissed anyone for a long time. I didn't intend to kiss you."

"It's all right," she assured him. "I didn't intend to kiss you, either. I didn't intend to drench your shirt for the second time, either."

He either coughed or chuckled, she couldn't tell which. He cleared his throat. "To be fair, there's something I have to tell you. Something I hope you'll keep to yourself." She heard him take a deep breath. "My—my wife died two years ago along with my infant son in a car crash."

She gasped. "I—I'm sorry."

"Don't be sorry for me. I've had enough sympathy to last a lifetime. I want to forget, that's all.

That's why I'm here. To get away from everyone who knows me and knows what happened. Who reminds me of what I've lost by just being kind or sympathetic or whatever. I don't know why I'm telling you this, but I had to explain why I blew it tonight. I'm not sure what happened to me, but I didn't want you to think I went around kissing women."

"No, of course not. And I wouldn't want you to think I went around crying on men's shoulders, because I don't."

"I'm sure you don't," he said.

"Well, now that we've settled that..." she said uneasily. She wasn't sure what, if anything, had been settled. "I appreciate your telling me. I'll keep it to myself."

"I hope you feel better," he said.

"Oh, yes, there's nothing like a good cry," she said. Or a good kiss. Her lips still tingled, her heart still pounded and he didn't seem to feel a thing. Except regret. If he did, he wasn't going to admit it. "I'm fine, really. I thought I was over it—the divorce, Jason, everything. I *am* over it. I just had a relapse. But now I'm fine," she repeated, more to convince herself than him.

"That's good," he said. "Please tell your aunt I enjoyed the dinner. That's the first decent meal I've had since I left San Francisco. She's a great cook and a wonderful hostess."

"Yes, she is, and she's been so good to Dylan and me. If it weren't for her, we'd be...well, we'd be up a creek. She liked you, too. She'll probably invite you again."

"That's very kind, but I couldn't accept. From

now on I'm staying on the ranch. That's why I bought it, to have a place to stay."

You mean hide out, she thought. "But maybe you need to get out and—"

"And make new friends? Mix with people? Stop living in the past? Is that what you're going to say? Believe me, I've heard it all. That's why I left California. I told you what happened to me because I thought you were different from other people. Because I thought you'd accept me as I am. A loner. A man who's lost the only woman he ever loved, the only woman he ever will love, who doesn't want to be dragged back into society. I guess I was wrong. You're just like everyone else. The truth is nobody who hasn't lost their whole family in the space of a second could possibly understand."

Laura stiffened. There was so much anger and bitterness in his voice, she could feel his pain. But he was right. It was true. She couldn't really understand how he felt. She could sympathize, but he didn't want her sympathy. It was hard to understand why any man wouldn't want to get on with his life—after a decent period of mourning, of course. But she'd never known true love the way he had. This was not an ordinary man. This was a sensitive, caring man who'd let her cry her heart out on his chest tonight. A man who must have been deeply in love with his wife. She'd never known that kind of love. For that she envied him.

"Good night, Laura," he said.

She hung up and started up the stairs when she heard her aunt's door open.

"Who was that?" Emily asked in a hushed voice, tying the sash on her robe.

"That was Brandon. He thinks you're a great cook."

"Is that all?"

"And a wonderful hostess."

"I mean, is that all he said."

"No. He explained his situation so I'd understand why he doesn't want to socialize."

"Doesn't want to socialize? That's ridiculous. I hope you told him so. No? Well, then I'll have to tell him."

"You do that, Aunt," Laura said, and climbed the stairs to her room. "If you get a chance," she murmured.

THE NEXT MORNING her heart felt as if it were made of lead when she thought about last night. She'd made a fool of herself with a man who was not interested in her and never would be. He would spend the rest of his life grieving for his wife and son. She'd never known such devotion. She couldn't fathom it. But she respected him for his loyalty. She just wished that her kisses meant something to him beside "blowing it." Because they meant something to her. How much she wasn't sure.

She got the message. He was going to bury himself on the ranch and hang a Do Not Disturb sign on his door and on his heart. The worst part was that she'd told him he didn't know anything about being a parent. That was before she knew about him, how it must have hurt. From now on she'd keep her mouth shut. And keep her distance.

After serving her guests breakfast trays in their rooms, Aunt Emily had gone off to the farmer's market on the edge of town. Laura and Dylan were eating flaky croissants at the table in the kitchen in her aunt's old-fashioned breakfast nook.

"Do dreams come true, Mom?" Dylan asked.

"They can come true if you believe in them. Why?"

"Cuz I had a dream last night that I want it to come true."

"What was it about?"

"It's a secret."

"I see. Well, sometimes you have to help your dreams come true. You have to do your part, and work to make them come true. For example, if you dreamed of having a new bike, you could find a way to earn the money for one. Or if you dreamed of being a fireman, then you did exercises and got strong and studied hard for the firefighters' exam, that would be doing your part. Do you understand?"

He nodded enthusiastically and her heart lightened. Everything was going to be all right, after all. "What are you going to do today?" she asked.

"Go over to Jeff's house."

Laura breathed a sigh of relief. Not a word about the ranch or his father or his tree house. Could her problems with Dylan be over? She was afraid to get her hopes up, but she smiled brightly. "We'll have to invite Jeff to do something with you on the weekend. Maybe go fishing at the reservoir," she suggested.

"Okay," he said, wiped his mouth on a napkin and took off out the back door. A little too fast. A little too eagerly. Laura watched him go, a tiny niggling worry at the back of her mind.

Chapter Six

Brandon stood on his deck watching the morning sun highlight the purple hills on the horizon. The air was so dry, so still, so full of the smells of dry grass and wild roses, he should have been energized. This was just what he'd pictured when he bought the ranch, sight unseen, based on the photos the Realtor had sent him. No sounds, no people, but no car, either. When he called Scotty's Garage a little earlier, they said the part wouldn't be in until tomorrow. So he was stuck there. But wasn't that what he'd wanted? To be stuck? To be isolated? Not when he knew he couldn't leave if he wanted to. Not if he couldn't leave without calling Laura and asking her to pick him up. The person he knew he must have antagonized by telling her she didn't understand him.

He could tell she was hurt by what he'd said on the phone last night. Now he knew he should never have confided in her in the first place. He had no idea what had gotten into him last night. First kissing her and then trying to explain it away. The truth was he couldn't explain it, not to her and not to himself. All he knew was that he'd let himself go. Part of the reason was simply that she was a desirable woman, soft and sweet with a core of strength he admired.

In fact, he admired everything about her—her dark hair, her amber eyes, her soft curves. Pressed against him, her lips soft and responsive, he'd lost control. Even now he wondered what would have happened if the phone hadn't rung. When would he have come to his senses and realized he was betraying the memory of his one true love?

No wonder he felt restless. He was trapped. Every time he tried to do some work, he thought about Laura. He thought about kissing her, about how he'd forgotten everything for a few moments. Forgotten Jeanne and how much he'd loved her. How he promised himself he'd never forget her. But he had forgotten. And that made him feel guilty.

Yes, he was stuck. But he shouldn't care. He had enough food and enough work to do. Then why didn't he do it? Why did he stand there staring at the vast fields where cows and horses once grazed? At least they were grazing in the pictures he'd seen. Why did he stand there and wonder what life was like when the McIntyres lived here, when it was a real working ranch, when the air was filled with the shouts of children, the house was filled with the smell of stew simmering on the back of the stove and bread baking in the oven?

He pictured Laura growing up there, riding horses across the field and climbing trees. He felt a deep sense of regret knowing that no more children would run across the fields, fish in the creek or climb the trees. At least not while he lived there. He wandered out to the tree house, looked up into the branches and saw... No it couldn't be, but it looked like Dylan's bare legs dangling over the edge of the tree house. He stood for a long moment telling himself he was imagining the whole thing. But he knew he wasn't.

"Dylan?"

"What?" The boy sounded surprised he'd been found. He jerked his legs back up into the tree house as if he could disappear and Brandon wouldn't know he'd been there.

"What are you doing up there?" Brandon asked calmly.

Dylan leaned forward and met his gaze. "Waiting for my dad."

As if Brandon didn't know. He took a deep breath and told himself to be patient, be understanding. As patient and understanding as if it were his own son.

"I thought we'd agreed you wouldn't wait for him anymore, not until we'd decided what to do with the tree house. At least not until it got repaired or there was an adult here with you. Me or your mom or..."

"I know. There is an adult coming. My dad. He's coming to get me today."

"Really. Your dad is coming to get you today? How do you know?"

"He told me. He told me to wait for him here. He's coming in his new car and he's bringing me a BB gun and a bow and arrow."

Brandon rocked back on his heels. The boy had an active imagination, but could this be true? Was his father coming back to get him? If *his* son was alive, there was nothing that could keep him away. Maybe Dylan's father felt the same way. Maybe he was on his way right now. It was possible he didn't know the whole story. Even Laura said there had been good times. But she didn't say his father was coming to get him. Maybe she didn't know. If she did, he was sure she wouldn't let him go.

"You know it's dangerous up there," Brandon said, eyeing the rotten boards and the rusty nails. "I wouldn't want you to fall down before your dad gets here."

"He's gonna fix it for me. He has all the stuff in the shed. He just didn't have time before he left cuz he had an important job to do."

"In the shed," Brandon repeated. "Why don't you show it to me? Maybe you and I can fix it."

"I can't. I gotta wait here. He's coming here to get me."

Brandon nodded. He didn't want to antagonize the kid. He just wanted to get him down. "I'm sure we'll hear his car. What was it, a Maserati?"

"A Porsche," Dylan said.

"They make a lot of noise coming up the drive at seven hundred RPM's," Brandon said soberly.

There was a long pause.

"Well, okay," Dylan said at last. "But first I'm gonna leave a note for him in my secret mailbox."

"Secret mailbox?" Brandon asked, looking around the tree house.

"It's in a hole in the tree," he said. "But I'm not telling where, cuz it's a secret. Could you get me some paper and a pencil?"

Brandon hesitated a moment. The boy was being so reasonable; how could he refuse such an innocent request? "Sure, I'll be right back."

He was back a few minutes later, he went halfway up the ladder with the paper and pencil, reached out as Dylan reached down to get them. Then he waited for another five minutes while Dylan composed his message.

''How do you spell *alone?*'' he asked.

Brandon told him.

''Is that the same as lonely?'' he asked.

''You can be alone and not be lonely,'' Brandon said. ''For example, you're alone up in your tree house, but you're feeling so happy, you don't feel lonely. Or you're in the middle of a crowd of people, but you still feel lonely. Do you understand what I mean?''

It was a hard concept for a little kid to grasp, one that had even been a painful concept for a grown man to grasp, but Dylan nodded gravely. Finally he finished his message, told Brandon to close his eyes and Dylan put the note in his secret mailbox.

''Ready?'' Brandon asked. ''Maybe we can fix your tree house before your dad comes.'' What was he saying? Laura had told him in no uncertain terms his father wasn't coming back. Brandon didn't want to fix the tree house. He wanted to get it off his property. But he was trapped. He couldn't possibly say no now. *One step at a time,* he told himself.

''Do you know how to fix things?'' Dylan asked skeptically.

''Some things.'' Memories came rushing back of their house in Marin County. The summer he'd spent his vacation from the securities firm he was working for in the city replacing a rotten redwood deck. He'd smashed his thumb, cut his hand, dropped a hammer on his toe, but he'd made a deck that was still standing when he sold the house. He remember the pride he'd felt, the pride that shone in Jeanne's eyes. A different pride than when he'd gotten his raise. Different from when he was made partner. Or when he made his first million. The deck was a concrete achievement. Maybe that's what he needed now. Another achievement he could see, touch and feel.

"If the stuff is in the shed, if you help me, I'm sure I can fix it. Come on down and show me where it is," Brandon said.

There was a long silence. Brandon could almost hear the wheels turning in the boy's head while he entertained second thoughts. Should he trust Brandon or not? If he left the tree house for only a moment, would he miss his dad? Finally he came flying down the ladder.

Together they headed for the shed behind the house. Brandon had never looked in it. He hadn't looked in the barn, either. Why bother? He had no use for outbuildings. Sure enough, in a weather-beaten shed there were sheets of plywood and two-by-fours stacked against the wall. There were power tools, saws and hammers and bins of nails and screws of all sizes. It was the workshop of a man who had plans, whether for a tree house or something bigger. There was enough material here to rebuild the tree house completely and then some.

"Think your dad would mind if we used his stuff?" Brandon asked. He didn't point out that it was now *his* stuff, that he'd bought the ranch and everything in it. All the furnishings and equipment. It was all his.

Dylan looked around at the boards, his forehead furrowed in a frown, as if he didn't know, wasn't sure what his father would say. Or maybe he preferred to do it with his dad as planned, and not the stranger who'd taken over his house and land. Brandon could understand that. Dylan didn't want a substitute dad, not even for a day. Brandon didn't want a substitute kid, either. He wanted one of his own. He wanted to teach his own kid—not somebody else's—to build, to read, to play soccer.

Brandon picked up the boards one by one, studying them for imperfections, running his hand along the sandpaper, checking the blade on the table saw while giving the boy time to think it over. If he said no, then Brandon was off the hook. He'd go back to the house, call Dylan's mother and tell her to come and get her son. After all, he didn't really want to build a tree house. Not here and not now. At one time he would have loved the opportunity. Not any longer.

Finally Dylan looked up at Brandon. "The tree house wasn't really mine. It's been there a long time. Since before I was born. I wanted to fix the roof so I could sleep there. My dad and I were gonna do that and repair the deck and stuff, cuz he wanted to teach me how to build things. We were gonna do it together. But he didn't have time. He was too busy."

Too busy running through your mother's money, Brandon thought. If the rumors were true. Dylan's stubborn lower lip stuck out defiantly as if he knew what Brandon was thinking, as if Brandon would dare to question his dad's good intentions.

"So, what do you think?" Brandon asked. "We could actually rebuild the tree house with a new roof and surprise your dad. You'll be up there in a tree house that's safe. That you made. He'll be proud of you."

Dylan nodded slowly. "Okay. If he comes we'll

prob'ly hear him, like you said. But even if we don't, he'll find my note I left him.''

The sun was strong now at midday, beating down on them as they hauled the boards out to the gravel driveway. Brandon was surprised how strong the kid was. He easily held up his end of the heavy boards. In the shade of the oak tree they set up a worktable made up of a slab of plywood on two sawhorses.

''What are we gonna do first?'' Dylan asked. His eyes were bright with hope and excitement. His gaze traveled from the worktable to the tree house and back again.

Brandon suddenly wavered. What was he doing? Oh, he could build a new tree house. They could do it together. But it would take longer than today. In the meantime the kid's hopes were rising. He was doing this because his dad was coming. What if he wasn't? Maybe he ought to call Laura before they began this project. He should have called her earlier. What if she didn't approve?

''First we'll have lunch,'' Brandon said. ''I'll go get us something and you can sort these nails and screws according to size.'' He held out a couple of coffee cans and Dylan sat on the front step of the house and diligently began to sort. ''Then we're going to tear down the rotten boards at the old tree house.''

He saw a wave of indecision cross they boy's face. He remembered how tearing down the tree house had not been an option for the boy, but Dylan finally nodded and went back to his task.

In the cool interior of the thick-walled house, Brandon went to his office, which was once the family room, and he saw the light on his answering machine flash. He was afraid it was Laura, but it was only messages from his clients. Clients he could take care of later. Laura had to know now. It was noon, so he called her aunt's house, but there was no answer. He called the post office and she answered. When she heard his voice, she said, ''Yes?'' in a cool voice.

''Dylan's here,'' he said.

''Oh, no. I'll be right there.''

''Wait a minute,'' he protested, but she hung up.

He called back, but someone else answered and said Laura was on her lunch break.

He proceeded to make two cheese sandwiches, got himself a beer and the kid a cola and went outside. Dylan's eyes lit up when he saw the soda. He said his mom didn't let him drink sodas. They were expensive, contained too much sugar and would eventually rot his teeth.

The two of them sat on the steps eating in silence. Brandon debated whether to tell Dylan his mother was on her way. If she hadn't been so upset, she might have listened to him explain the situation. Then she wouldn't have had to dash out there. But she did dash out there. Her truck coughed and sputtered its way down the driveway.

Dylan's eyes widened. ''I'm in trouble,'' he muttered, wiping his mouth with the back of his hand. ''I'm not s'posed to be here and I'm not s'posed to be drinking a soda.''

''Maybe I can explain,'' Brandon said. He knew how she'd look, her hair flying, her eyes blazing, ready to grab her son. So he ambled over and met her at her truck to head her off, to get a chance to say a few words before she exploded, which she looked like she was ready to do.

"Where is he?" she demanded, her hand on the door handle of the truck. "As if I didn't know. He's in the tree house, isn't he? After our deal. After he promised." Her lower lip trembled. He couldn't let her cry again. Not here in this driveway. He knew what might happen. He couldn't take a chance.

He leaned against the door, blocking her way, trapping her inside the truck. "Just a second. He's not in the tree house. He came down. He says his dad is coming to get him."

"That's what he always says. I told you he's not coming." She turned the door handle, but he put his hand over hers. He wasn't going to let her out. Not until she understood what was happening.

"But this time he seems more certain. He says his father told him he'd come today. Is that possible?" Brandon asked.

"No, of course not. Where is he? Let me talk to him. He can't come out here. He can't use his tree house."

"Calm down, will you?" he asked.

"Calm down?" She pulled her hand away from his. "You're telling me to calm down? You're the one who doesn't want him here. It's your ranch, remember? You don't want anyone to come here and you don't want to go anywhere. You want to be alone." Her face was flushed, her hair curled in tendrils around her face, her mouth was set in a straight line. The same mouth that had kissed him last night. If he kissed her again, right now, he knew how her lips would feel. She'd resist at first and then her mouth would soften, mold to his… A shaft of desire hit him right in the core of his body. It wasn't going to happen. Not the way it had yesterday.

He had no excuse to touch her. She was off-limits. She thought he was a recluse. A hermit. That was what he wanted her to think. But that was yesterday. Now, seeing her behind the wheel of her truck, looking small and vulnerable, her eyes flashing warning signals, he knew why he'd offered to help Dylan make a new tree house.

Yes, he was concerned with the boy's safety. Yes, he enjoyed working with his hands. Yes, he felt sorry for the kid. But those were not the real reasons he'd done it. The real reason was so he could see Laura again. So he'd have an excuse to see her. So she'd have to drive out here and she'd have to talk to him, look at him with those beautiful eyes. So he could have an excuse to touch her, to put his hand on hers.

The truth hit him like a massive two-by-four in the middle of the chest. The reason he was doing this. He knew what it was and he was ashamed of himself. He might admit it to himself, but he'd never admit it to her. He told himself it was lust, pure and simple. Lust he couldn't help. Lust because it had been so long. Such a long time not looking at women, not noticing the color of their eyes or the curl in their hair or the way their skirt hugged their trim little bottom. Or the lace of their underwear.

He realized she was looking at him, a look that said she knew what he was thinking. But how could she? It wasn't possible. Their eyes locked and held for a long moment. Then she pushed against the truck door. "Let me out of here," she said breathlessly. When what she really meant was "Quit looking at me like that."

"In a minute. He was in the tree house this morning. I didn't want him up there in danger of breaking his neck when the thing fell apart, so I told him I'd help him rebuild it. We found some materials in the shed and we took them. I hope you don't mind." The last thing he wanted to do was to remind her that nothing here was hers anymore.

"Mind? Do I mind?" She looked dazed. "Those were materials Jason bought to build a deck for a hot tub, but as with all of his plans—" She broke off, blinked and managed a quavery smile. "Don't worry, I'm not going to cry. He's not worth crying over."

Brandon reached into his back pocket and pulled out a handkerchief. "Just in case," he said as he handed it to her.

She nodded. "Thank you. You can let me out now. I'm not going to skin him alive the way I planned. I don't blame him for trying to find his dad. I blame myself. It's my fault he doesn't have his dad here. I just don't understand why he came now, today."

Brandon opened the door for her and took her arm to help her out. Her eyes widened. Surprised at that simple gesture. Why? What kind of men was she used to? What was her husband like besides being a no-good, no-account, rotten bastard who ran through all her money? Unreliable? Undependable? Impolite? Just the brush of her warm skin against his caused his heart to race out of control. Lust, he reminded himself. That's all it is.

Laura jumped down from the truck, her legs unsteady. She'd raced out here determined to grab Dylan by the scruff of his neck and haul him away. She was prepared for an argument with Brandon. But he'd taken the wind out of her sails by being so damned nice. Too bad he was so damned unavailable. Oh, well, she had enough to worry about without falling for the new man in town.

"Dylan, what are you doing here?" she asked, standing over him with her hands on her hips.

He looked up at her, his blue eyes defiant. "I'm gonna build a new tree house."

"But I told you you couldn't do that," she said.

"You told me I had to help my dreams come true," he said. "I dreamed that my dad was coming to get me. So I came out here. That's what you said. That's what you told me. I could help make my dream come true."

"Oh, Dylan." What could she say? That's what she'd told him.

"The workers are on their lunch break," Brandon said, sitting down on the gravel next to Dylan. "Care to join us?"

She stared down at them, both chewing hungrily, surrounded by hammers, nails and boards and shook her head. In an ideal world, this was the way it was. Man and boy working together on a project. Bonding. Learning from each other. But this was the wrong man. The right man had never built anything. Never spent time with the boy. Except in the boy's dreams.

How long would this man spend with the boy who so badly needed a father, a mentor? A few hours? And then what? The boy is left in the lurch again, forgotten and disappointed. And what was going to happen when the boy's father didn't show up today the way he said he would in Dylan's dream? What could she do but give up and be grateful for small favors. Brandon had not ordered him off the property. Brandon was going to fix the tree house. Which would make it even more attractive to Dylan. How then would she keep him away from it? But this wasn't the time to bring that up. This was the time to leave.

"Thank you, but I have to get back to work. I can't come back until five." She looked at Dylan and then at Brandon, waiting for one or both of them to protest, saying it was too soon or too late, but Dylan shrugged and Brandon just nodded.

"I'll be here," Brandon said. "I'm stuck. My car won't be ready today."

Not knowing what else to say, Laura left them there eating their lunch on the ground, feeling strangely excluded and worried about the consequences of this strange turn of events.

Back in the post office she took advantage of a lull in business to telephone her aunt and explain the situation.

"I don't understand," her aunt said. "Brandon Marsh is actually building a new tree house for Dylan? On his ranch?"

"No. Yes. He's doing it so he can get Dylan out of his hair."

"That doesn't make sense," Emily said.

"I think he believes I can't keep Dylan away from the tree house. That I have no control over him. Which seems to be true. Honestly, I don't know what else to do. I've threatened Dylan and bribed him. Since Brandon is afraid the tree house is dangerous in its present condition, he's making it safe. He's probably afraid of the liability. I don't know what will happen next. The best thing would be if I get the job at the post office and take over Willa Mae's apartment, then we could move the tree house to the back yard. But Dylan wouldn't accept that. He thinks his daddy is coming to the ranch to get him. That's what he dreamed last night. In any case, I'm going there after work to pick him up, so I'll be late for dinner."

"Why don't I pack a hamper for you to take out there for supper? The man seemed to like my cooking."

"Of course he did," Laura said. "Everyone likes your cooking, but that doesn't mean—"

"I have some leftover cornmeal-crusted chicken and marinated vegetables and some brownies. After a hard day's work a man gets hungry."

Laura half expected her to say something about the way to a man's heart. She didn't, but if she knew her aunt, that's what she was thinking. She also knew her feelings would be hurt if she didn't accept her offer.

"I'll pack plenty, so of course you'll stay and eat with him."

"No, I couldn't do that, Aunt Emily. It would be too awkward. He'd think—"

"What would he think? That you're showing your appreciation, that's all, for taking Dylan all day. And that I enjoy cooking for people, especially for attractive men. And that you enjoy eating with someone your age instead of with a dotty old aunt and your son."

"But I don't want—I just want to pick up Dylan and get out of there. That's what he wants, too. He wants to be left alone. That's what he told me."

"Hmmpf." Her aunt sniffed. "I've never met a man yet who didn't appreciate a good meal, and that includes Mr. Marsh. I'll have the basket packed by five, so you come by and pick it up. If he turns you down I'll eat my chef's hat."

Laura reluctantly agreed, fearing that this was her aunt's way of throwing her niece together with the most eligible man to ever arrive in Silverado, not knowing that he wasn't eligible at all. Laura couldn't tell her Brandon's tragic story, though maybe she already knew. But it wasn't Laura's wish to spread any gossip that Brandon had told her in confidence and that would make people feel sorry for him. Brandon had been adamant in his refusal to accept any sympathy from anyone. She wasn't going to waste any on him.

On the way to the ranch she decided how she'd handle the food her aunt had sent. Once she'd arrived and had thanked Brandon for his help, she'd shoo Dylan into the truck and then casually hand Brandon the picnic hamper. He might say, "Why don't you stay and eat with me?" and she'd say "No, thanks, we have to be getting back." She wasn't going to stay any longer than absolutely necessary. Her aunt might not believe her, but Brandon didn't want company. He might want food, but he didn't want people. No matter how amiable he seemed at the moment. His amiability could be attributed directly to the fact that she was taking Dylan home and he could be alone at last.

But Dylan wasn't standing in the driveway waiting for her as she'd pictured. She had to follow the sound of pounding to the driveway in front of the garage. There she found Dylan hammering nails into a two-by-four and Brandon lifting a huge sheet of plywood off the sawhorses. She stood there for a long moment watching, neither of them aware of her presence. Her son's face was flushed and his lower lip was caught by his teeth as he concentrated on his task.

Instead of well-pressed designer blue jeans and a yuppie polo shirt with a logo on it, Brandon was now wearing a faded T-shirt and denim cutoffs. His arms and muscular legs had tanned in the Nevada sun in the brief time he'd spent at the ranch, and sweat beaded on his forehead. This was obviously a man who did not spend all his time sitting in front of a computer. Those muscles had not developed overnight.

She stood rooted to the spot, her gaze moving from his broad shoulders to his torso and down his legs. Her pulse raced. A flight of butterflies took up residence in her stomach. She tried to tear her eyes away, but she couldn't. She couldn't have been more surprised at the transformation of a city man than if he'd suddenly appeared in leather chaps and a Stetson. When he ripped a rusty nail from a board with the back of a hammer, she felt like he was ripping away at a protective cover she'd put around herself months ago. She shook herself and took a deep breath. She had to do something, say something to break the spell.

"Hello."

Brandon dropped his hammer and looked up at her.

She forgot her plan and just to have something to do, something to say, she held out the basket in front of her. "Compliments of my aunt," she said briskly.

"What's in it, Mom?" Dylan asked.

''Just some food for Mr. Marsh,'' she said.

Brandon corrected her. ''Brandon,'' he said, straightening and walking up to her. He lifted the wicker cover and looked inside. ''Fried chicken. Looks good. How did she know it was my favorite food?''

''Mine, too,'' Dylan said.

''Come on, Dylan. We're going home. You've taken up quite enough of Mr. Marsh—I mean Brandon's time. Say thank you.''

''Thank you, Brandon,'' he said dutifully, but his eyes never left the picnic basket. Dylan seemed more interested in the contents of the basket than in their imminent departure.

''And homemade biscuits and a three-bean salad and brownies if I'm not mistaken,'' Brandon said, lifting a checkered cloth.

''Brownies!'' Dylan exclaimed. ''She never makes those for us.''

''Dylan. Not another word. We're going home to dinner.''

''We don't got a home,'' he said, giving her that look that said it all, that made her feel like the worst parent in the world.

She grabbed his hand and pulled him toward the truck, but he yanked at her arm, resisting every step of the way.

''Wait a minute,'' Brandon said. ''There's plenty of food here. Why don't you stay and eat here? But maybe you have somewhere to go.''

''Yes,'' Laura said.

''No,'' Dylan said.

''Oh, all right,'' Laura said, exasperated. Brandon was obviously being polite, and she was so tired of saying no to Dylan that she dropped his hand and let him hop up and down joyously. What harm could it do, after all, to spend an hour eating dinner if it meant so much to her son? On the other hand, Brandon was here for the solitude, not to entertain the former owners of his ranch. It was obvious he was just being polite. Her aunt had sent the food, enough for an army. What could he do but offer to share it with them? Which her deviously clever aunt knew full well.

They ate on the picnic table on the deck, the one her grandfather made from a pine tree that fell over in a windstorm one winter. Dylan never stopped talking. She'd never seen him so excited, so full of enthusiasm for a project. He talked about the improvements they were making to the tree house, the roof and the window and the shelf to keep his toys. And a secret place to hide messages and his own treasures. He ate some chicken, then took a brownie and went off to look for arrowheads in the Indian mound behind the house. He'd found one once, which he kept in the old cigar box with his other treasures.

Suddenly it was very quiet at the table. She shouldn't have let Dylan go off like that. She should have packed up the empty dishes and left. But it seemed rude to eat and run, especially when Brandon was still eating. She had to say that he appeared to really enjoy her aunt's picnic. Her aunt would be smug when she heard that, especially when she heard that he'd shared it with them. Which she obviously hoped would happen.

Laura gazed out at the purple sagebrush and thought about other dinners out here, her parents, grandparents, neighbors, gathered together on this big, old veranda, as it was called then, enjoying pot-luck dinners at this table, watching the children at play. The men would smoke their cigars out here and the women would go into the kitchen to do the dishes.

"Would you like some coffee?" he said at last.

Startled, she turned abruptly. "Oh, no, we have to get going," she said.

"I'm going to make some," he said, unfolding his long legs from the bench.

"If you'll show me where the fuse box is. I blew a fuse today with the electric saw."

"It's in the pantry," she said, accompanying him into the kitchen. It was dark in the kitchen, but she didn't need any light. She'd know her way around if she was blindfolded. He followed her into the pantry. The small, dark room still smelled of pickles and relishes and preserves as it always had and always would, even though she'd cleaned everything out. Waves of nostalgia came washing over her. She should never have come back here. It was too painful.

She was intensely aware of Brandon's presence, only inches away from her. The outline of his body was all she could see, but she knew how broad his shoulders were, how his hair fell over his forehead and how his skin had tanned to a golden bronze from working outside. How he didn't look so much like a city dweller anymore. She tried not to notice, but she couldn't help herself. She was drawn to him as she'd never been drawn to any man. That didn't mean she was helpless. She could fight it. She had to fight it. She had no choice.

"Wait," Brandon said, grabbing her arm as she reached for the fuse box.

Her heart stalled, her pulse rate skyrocketed. She tried to pull her arm away, but he held on to her.

"I have to tell you," he said. "I was way out of line last night. I had no business going off like that about my troubles. You're the one who deserves sympathy, not me. You've lost your house, everything. I want to make it up to you."

"There's no need," she said, fighting to stay calm, to breathe normally. "Everything that happened to me is my fault. I have no one to blame but myself. I just got what I deserved."

"I don't believe that. I don't believe anyone deserves to lose their house and their security. Especially not you. You're too—" He traced the outline of her cheek with the pad of his thumb and she trembled all over. His touch was unbelievably tender for such a gruff man. "You're too good and you're too beautiful," he said as his voice dropped to a whisper. His lips were only a breath away from hers. She felt the heat shimmy up her spine. His lips covered hers and a roaring filled her ears.

It wasn't lightning, it wasn't thunder and it wasn't an earthquake. They were in a desert valley where those things didn't happen. But she could have sworn she'd been struck by lightning. No man's kiss could do what his did. Could make the lights flash and the ground shake beneath her feet. Could cause her to kiss him back. To make her throw her arms around his neck and hang on for dear life.

They came up for air after the longest, deepest kiss she'd ever known, and he nuzzled the sensitive spot behind her ear. In the back of her mind she knew she ought to leave. She feared another scene in which Brandon was overcome with guilt. A person didn't get over those feelings in a hurry. Some people never did. He said he was one of them. She believed him. Then why would she allow herself to fall for a man who would never fall for her? She wouldn't.

"I have to go," she murmured.

Reluctantly he dropped his arms and let her go. She managed to pull herself together just enough to find the fuse box and flip the switch. The light blinded her. She blinked and avoided his gaze. Then she left the pantry, hurried through the kitchen and outside. She grabbed the picnic basket and called Dylan. While she was waiting for him, Brandon put Dylan's bike in the back of her truck.

"Dylan wants to come back tomorrow," Brandon said. "to help finish the tree house. I didn't know how you'd feel about it so I didn't say yes or no."

"How I'd feel about it?" Had she heard right? Surely he wasn't willing to have Dylan there another day. "You're the one who has to put up with him. I don't want him to be burden. After all, you have your own work to do."

"My work will keep. We've got to get this tree house fixed before somebody gets hurt."

A dozen questions popped into her head. Like, And then what? What will Dylan do? What will you do about the tree house once it's fixed? She didn't need to verbalize them. He answered without her speaking a word.

"By then you'll hopefully know where you want the house. I'll have it moved wherever you say."

"That's very kind of you," she said. What else could she say? She could say that Dylan would be heartbroken if the tree house was moved because then this father couldn't find him, but why start that again. Instead she managed a stiff smile and told Brandon to call her when his car was ready, otherwise she'd be by tomorrow evening after work to pick up Dylan.

In a matter-of-fact tone he said he would, but his gaze was anything but matter-of-fact. He looked at her, and she saw something that disturbed her. She saw needs and wants and simmering seduction there. And that shocked her. This was a man who'd lost his one true love. But still a man. A man who was struggling to fight off an attraction to her. A man who'd just given in to that attraction in a moment of weakness.

This was a man who'd never fall in love again. He'd made that clear. He had no more love to give because his love had been given away and had died with his wife and child. It was just as well. She was in no position to get attached to anyone right now. But was she attracted to him? She had to admit she was. Who wouldn't be?

He was rich, he was good-looking and he'd been incredibly kind to her son even though he didn't want him around. And there was more. There was something else, something she couldn't define—call it chemistry, call it electricity. She could call it anything she wanted, but she couldn't deny it. Not anymore. That didn't mean she had to fall into the man's arms every time the lights went out. Because she had a son to raise, a job to get and a heart to protect to keep from getting hurt again.

"HOW DID HE like the chicken?" her aunt asked, greeting her niece in the living room when she returned.

"Very much," Laura said.

"Of course he asked you to stay and eat it with him," her aunt said with a smug smile.

"Yes, he did, how could he not?" Laura said. "And your chicken was delicious. I'll have to get the recipe."

"Of course. Tell me, is there anything really wrong with this man?" her aunt asked, not put off a bit by Laura's changing the subject to her cooking. "That the love of a good woman couldn't cure?"

"No, but—"

"I know about the accident that killed his wife and child," her aunt said. "Buzz told me."

"Good heavens, I hope the whole town doesn't know. He doesn't want pity."

"What *does* he want?" Emily asked, giving her niece a long look that made Laura feel as though Emily could see right through her. That she knew exactly what had happened tonight.

"To be left alone," Laura said flatly. It was time her aunt got rid of her romantic notions.

"Then why have Dylan around?" Emily asked.

"I don't know, Aunt Emily," Laura said, shaking her head. "I don't really understand the man. I think sometimes he doesn't understand himself. He's a stranger here in a strange land. He doesn't know our history or anything about us. And we know nothing about him. Except maybe a few things." Like how he kisses. Like the way he looks at me, like I was a kind of forbidden fruit, and how he looks at Dylan with a kind of distant longing. How he makes me feel.... How he's afraid to feel.... Oh, Lord, she was so tired, tired of making excuses for herself, for him....

TWO DAYS WENT BY, days filled with thoughts of the stranger who lived in her house. Dylan rode his bike to the ranch in the morning and she picked him up at night. Laura didn't bring another picnic hamper, although her aunt strongly suggested it, and Brandon didn't invite her to stay for dinner. In fact, she barely saw him and hardly spoke to him. He seemed just as anxious as she to avoid any further contact that might lead to unwanted intimacy. Just as sorry as she that he'd given in to temptation. What else was new? The man was full of contradictions and so, she had to admit, was she.

Though Brandon kept their conversation to a minimum—no, his car wasn't ready and no, he didn't need anything—Dylan talked endlessly about what they were doing, how they'd replaced the rotten boards and how Brandon had let Dylan use the saw and taught him to use the Phillips-head screwdriver. Strangely enough Dylan never said a word about his father. Though that was obviously the reason he was there. To rebuild the tree house so he could safely wait there for him. He didn't ask why his father hadn't come yet or when he'd be there. Yet Laura was afraid that his faith in Jason's return was not diminished one bit.

She found out one evening after dinner that she was right.

Chapter Seven

''My dream didn't come true,'' Dylan said, shooting his mother an accusing look as he swung back and forth in the swing on her aunt's front porch. ''You said if I helped, it would. But my daddy still hasn't come back.''

''I know,'' Laura said, leaning against a post on the wide veranda. ''But some dreams just don't come true. No matter how much we want them to. No matter how hard we try. When I was about your age I dreamed of being a rodeo star. I practiced riding my pony bareback, round and round the corral, roping tree stumps, but my dream still didn't come true.''

''Instead you got to be a post office lady.''

She smiled wryly. It must sound pretty grim to an eight-year-old. At the moment it even sounded grim to her.

''What do you dream of now?'' he asked, stopping the swing with the toe of his sneaker and cocking his head at her.

''Right now? I dream of being the postmistress and getting the apartment over the post office for us, with the fenced yard in back. And I'm doing everything I can to make that dream come true. I work hard at my job and...and...well, I'm just waiting to hear.'' Okay, maybe it didn't sound like much of a dream to an eight-year-old, but there were times when you realized that certain dreams weren't going to come true, like happily-ever-after, and you'd better lower your expectations and substitute something more realistic.

''But when my dream comes true, you won't need your dream anymore, Mom. You won't need to work at the post office and we can move back to the ranch,'' he said.

She swallowed hard. Was this the time to tell him once again that his daddy wasn't coming back? No, it wasn't. If only dreams like his came true. She held her breath, waiting for Dylan to tell her they were going back to the ranch when his dream came true, but he didn't say that. If he had, she wouldn't have been able to stand it.

''Brandon said I got to be patient,'' he said. ''Do you know what that means?''

''Yes, I think I do,'' she said. ''It means your dream may take a long time to come true. But mine won't. It's going to come true very soon. At least I think it will.''

''Do you like him?'' her son asked.

''Who?'' she asked, startled.

''Brandon.''

''Yes, of course,'' she said quickly. What else could she say? How could she not like the man who, in spite of himself, was being good to her son?

''He likes you.''

She flushed, glad her son couldn't see her face in the dusk. She wanted to ask how he knew, but she didn't.

"He hasn't got a wife or a kid. We haven't got a dad." He paused and looked her in the eye.

Oh, Lord. How long did it take him to put two and two together. How many other people, like her aunt, were thinking the same thing?

"That's right," she said. "But we've got each other."

Dylan gave her a pitying look that said she had missed the point. So she had. But she'd missed it on purpose.

"He likes our house, too," Dylan continued. "And he's got a cool computer," Dylan said. "Can we get a computer?"

"Yes, sure, someday." She said, willing to promise him anything if he'd only change the subject. She'd almost added, *when we move into our new place,* but she'd said that so many times, it had lost its meaning.

"I played a game on it," Dylan continued.

"Really?" She tried to picture it, Brandon taking the time to show her son how to use his computer. Where did he get the computer game? She tried to imagine why Brandon was going out of his way to be nice to her son. A son who must remind him of the son he'd lost. Building the tree house, she could understand. It was a way of eventually getting rid of the house and of Dylan.

"I thought you were building the tree house," she said.

"Yeah, but sometimes it gets hot outside and he has to do some work inside. So I go in, too, and he talks on the phone and I play on his computer. He said it was okay, long as I don't talk and bother him.

That's how I know he likes you. I heard him say so."

"Who was he talking to?" she asked, more puzzled than ever.

"Somebody. I dunno. He said, 'She's nice.'"

"But how do you know he was talking about me?"

"I just know, that's all." With that he got up and went in to watch a rerun of a TV sitcom with her aunt. That was another good thing. Dylan had stopped complaining about her aunt. Maybe he was following Brandon's advice and becoming more patient. Patient with her aunt and patient with her. She could only hope so.

The next day she got the letter she'd been waiting for. The return address was the personnel department of the main post office. Taking advantage of the lull in business, she eagerly ripped the envelope open. And her heart fell. She had not gotten the job. She braced herself against the counter. Instead of the job of postmaster they were offering her the newly created job of rural delivery agent. A postmaster from a town fifty miles away with more experience was being transferred to Silverado to take the job she wanted. The job she deserved. The job she was supposed to get. And she was being given a vehicle and a route. She bit her lip to keep from crying out and reread the letter.

It slowly sank into her brain—her job, the job she was counting on, the job that was meant for her, was being given to someone else. She read on. But *but*—they were pleased to offer her the new job at her current rank and salary, for which, they felt she was better suited than for the postmaster job. Due to the high demand from rural customers, the new delivery service was going to be inaugurated this summer.

She read and reread the letter and each time reached the same conclusion. She would have gotten the job of postmistress if they hadn't created the new job. They couldn't let her go. They had to find her a job, but not the job she wanted. The reason they created the new job was because somebody complained about the lack of delivery service. That person was Brandon.

Just as she was fuming about that, Willa Mae, the former postmistress, who was dressed in a black T-shirt proclaiming Reno The Biggest Little City In The World and stretch pants and mules, shuffled into the post office from the upstairs apartment Laura had counted on inheriting from her. Which would now, by custom, go to the new man.

"Willa Mae, I haven't seen you for days," Laura said, resolutely planting a smile on her face.

"Been over to Reno with my sister, finding a place to live, getting ready for the big move. I had to come back for the Fourth. They don't know how to celebrate in Reno. Not like we do here. What's new down here in the office?"

Laura told her the news.

"Oh, my," Willa Mae said. "I was just sure you'd get the job. And move into my apartment. I was even going to leave my African violets for you. Now I think I'll take them with me. Unless you have a place for them...."

"I don't. I don't even have a place for myself and Dylan." She choked back feelings of self-pity. She wouldn't cry, not in front of Willa Mae, not in front of anybody.

"Never thought I'd see the day when we'd have delivery service anywhere around Silverado," Willa Mae said, shaking her head. "What's wrong with folks? They can't mosey into town to pick up their mail? Not that it wouldn't be a hoot, driving all over hell and gone delivering the mail." She grinned toothily at Laura. "Pulling over for a cup of coffee from a thermos, eating lunch along the road somewhere. And keeping tabs on who's doing what and where. Why, if I'd known that kind of thing was in the works, I might not have retired quite so soon. What kinda truck they gonna get you, four-wheel drive?"

"I don't know," Laura said dolefully, rubbing her hand over her aching forehead, wishing she could have half the enthusiasm Willa Mae had. Wondering if some day she'd be living alone in a small apartment in town, just like Willa Mae, or seeking out the bright lights of a big town.

She told herself she should be glad she had a job at all. That she might possibly enjoy being outside driving down country roads more than being inside the post office, staring out at the stores across the street. But she'd counted on the extra money, and more than that, she'd counted on the low-rent housing on the second floor. Where on earth was she going to live?

"What's this I hear about the man who bought your place?" Willa Mae asked, leaning against the counter.

"What did you hear?" Laura asked.

"That he's rich as Rockefeller and twice as good-looking. True?"

Laura smiled. She didn't know what to say. If she

agreed, it would be all over town and if she disagreed, well...

"Just my luck," Willa Mae said taking Laura's silence for an affirmative. "An eligible man comes to town just as I'm about to leave. And I haven't even met him yet."

"I'll introduce you the next time he comes in," Laura promised. "Then you can decide if he's twice as good-looking as a Rockefeller."

"If he is, I might decide not to leave," Willa Mae declared. "You know what they say about a good man being hard to find." She tilted her head to one side and observed Laura critically. "You look a little peaked," she pronounced. "I'll run up and fetch you a glass of my apricot cordial."

"Oh, no, I can't drink on the job," she said, but Willa Mae was out the door before she'd finished her sentence. And the phone rang.

"My car is ready," Brandon said. "I don't want to impose on you, but if you're free after work, Scotty will be there until six."

"Of course," she said, while inside she wanted to blurt out the bad news. She wanted to yell and scream at the unfairness of life, but she didn't. She said she'd be by after work to take him to town.

EVEN WHEN SHE ARRIVED at the ranch she couldn't say anything. About anything. Dylan was jumping up and down, excited to show her how he'd painted the boards that would be the new sides of the tree house. Still blithely unaware that the tree house would not be going back up the same tree. Still even more unaware that there was absolutely no place for the tree house to go at all. Or for them to live.

The three of them were tightly wedged in the front seat of the truck on the way back to the garage in town. Dylan between the adults, and Brandon's arm casually resting along the back of the seat. Laura could feel his fingers graze her shoulder, making shivers go up her spine even in the summer heat. Fortunately Dylan talked nonstop, so she didn't have to say a word. When he spotted his friend Andy on Main Street, Laura let him out to join him. Laura agreed Dylan could have dinner at Andy's house.

"You're quiet today," Brandon remarked to her as they pulled up across the street from Scotty's Garage. "Anything wrong?"

"You might say that," she said, her jaw clenched and her head throbbing. "You might also say that everything's wrong. For me. Not for you. For you, you got your wish."

He leaned against the passenger door, so relaxed and at ease, it made her more tense than ever. He shot her a puzzled look. For all the time he'd been without his beloved car, she thought he'd leap out of the truck and race over to pick it up at long last. Instead he just sat there, as if he'd forgotten he had a car, watching her and patiently waiting for her to explain.

"I didn't get the job of postmistress," she blurted. Strange, but just telling him seemed to make some of the hurt dissipate.

"I'm sorry," he said.

"So am I."

"What will you do?" he asked.

"Do? I'll tell you what I'm going to do," she said, gripping the steering wheel with white-knuckled fingers. "I'm going to be the new rural delivery person.

I'm going to drive a truck or a van or something all day and deliver your mail to your house at the ranch and every other ranch around here every day. What do you think of that?''

''I think it's great. You weren't meant to be cooped up in that office all day,'' he said.

''Maybe not. But I was meant to have the apartment over the post office, which traditionally goes to the postmaster. Now, because someone complained about the lack of door-to-door service out to the rural areas...''

''Wait a minute.'' He put his hand on her shoulder. ''Are you talking about me? Are you blaming me for your not getting the job you wanted?''

''Well...''

''Well, nothing,'' he said. ''I'm sorry about the apartment, but I never saw you as a postmistress.''

''Really. What did you see me as?'' she asked, her chin tilted up, her tone challenging him to come up with something. She wanted to make a grand gesture and remove his hand from her shoulder, but somehow she couldn't do that. It felt too good to have his hand there, too warm and too comforting—in spite of everything.

Brandon took his time thinking of an answer. He gave her a long look, admiring the way her hair fell to her shoulders, the way her white blouse covered her breasts and tempted him to reach over and unbutton it, right here on Main Street. He wondered what she'd do. He imagined the way her cheeks would turn scarlet, her heart would pound.

He imagined the scandal it would cause and he tried like hell to stifle the idea but it just wouldn't be stifled. He couldn't tear his eyes away from those buttons, couldn't stop imagining how she'd look without the blouse, without the lace bra he knew she was wearing. Now it was his heart that was pounding. And he hadn't touched her.

He realized at that moment he'd dreamed about her last night and in his dream she was wearing a black dress. No buttons. Just a long, smooth black dress. That was all he remembered. He wished he hadn't remembered any of it. Wished he'd repressed the whole thing. It was disturbing.

If he dreamed of anyone, he should dream about his wife, but he had no control over his dreams. He wondered if Laura had a black dress and where she'd wear it if she had one. It was easier to imagine her in a T-shirt and shorts. A T-shirt that clung to her breasts and shorts that exposed her long legs.

He dragged his gaze from the row of buttons on her blouse back to her face. He had no business fantasizing about this woman. Or any woman. He believed there was one woman for every man, and Jeanne had been his. But lately he'd had trouble picturing her face. It must be the move. The change of scene. The change of climate and geography. It had messed with his head. Since the day he'd arrived, he'd started changing. The worst part was he didn't know how far these changes would go.

Laura was angry. He knew that by the way her eyes blazed and her cheeks were stained with color. He was sorry she was angry with him. But he didn't think it was justified.

"What do I see you as?" he said at last, when he'd dredged his mind for the question she was waiting to hear the answer to. "I see you as a rodeo star, in a star-spangled outfit, riding bareback around the ring.'' Talk about fantasies. There was one that sent a shaft of pure desire through him. Laura in tights and spangles. Oh, Lord.

She stared at him, openmouthed, then a reluctant smile tugged at the corners of her mouth. ''Oh, I get it. Dylan told you, didn't he?''

''Told me what?'' he asked, feigning innocence.

''My childhood dream of becoming a rodeo star. I never rode that well and I'm certainly not the spangled type. It was a totally ridiculous dream.''

''Not as ridiculous as mine,'' he said. ''I wanted to be a race car driver.''

''You've almost succeeded,'' she said dryly. ''Didn't you say your car goes one hundred twenty?''

''Supposedly. But I'm not planning to race it. I gave up that dream a long time ago.'' He glanced up to see an older woman in a black T-shirt waving both hands at them from the sidewalk. ''Friend of yours?'' he asked.

Laura turned. ''That's Willa Mae, the former postmistress. She wants to meet you. I hope you don't mind.''

He muttered something unintelligible, something that gave her the impression he'd rather have a root canal than meet another of Silverado's colorful characters, but he got out of the truck and allowed Laura to introduce him to Willa Mae. He shook her bony hand, gave her an engaging smile and said he was happy to meet her.

''So, young fellow, how do you like it here?'' she asked, sizing him up with her bright blue gaze. ''People treating you right?'' she asked, shifting her gaze to Laura and back to him again.

Brandon assured her he liked it fine and that everyone was treating him very well. Laura noticed him sneaking a look at his watch, no doubt wondering if the garage would close before he picked up his car while he was standing out here making conversation.

''Would you like to come by for a glass of apricot cordial?'' Willa Mae asked Brandon with a coquettish smile. ''I made it myself.''

''You really should,'' Laura said, feeling slightly devilish. ''It's delicious.''

''If I weren't in a hurry to pick up my car at the garage,'' Brandon said, ''I'd take you up on your offer. Maybe I could have a rain check.''

''Oh, it never rains in Silverado,'' Willa Mae explained. ''Well, hardly ever. Except for the flash flood of '67. But before I leave I'll have you both up to my place. While it's still my place.''

Laura watched Brandon smoothly excuse himself and go into the service department of Scotty's garage. No wonder Willa Mae's wide-eyed gaze followed him as he crossed the street. The man knew how to turn on the charm. Then Willa Mae turned to give her report on the new man in town.

''Well, I must say, he's something, all right. Did I hear right? Is it possible he's available?'' she asked, licking her lips.

Laura didn't know what to say without giving away Brandon's past. ''Uh, well, I—he isn't married, if that's what you mean.''

''Darn tootin' that's what I mean. What are you doing, just standing there? Don't be shy. Go after him. 'Course if you're not interested, if you don't want him...I might... Say, there he goes,'' she exclaimed as Brandon's car pulled out of the garage and headed toward the highway. "What a car. What a man."

Laura pressed her lips together to keep from smiling. For years, Willa Mae had been the quintessential postmistress, hardworking and sensible, but ever since she'd announced her retirement, she'd been kicking up her heels, entertaining every single man in town, plying them with her homemade cordials in her digs above the post office. Is that what would happen to her? Man-crazy and desperate at sixty-five? It was a chilling thought.

Fortunately the tree house project seemed to go on and on into the next week, keeping Dylan occupied and happy. Laura wanted to ask Brandon if Dylan was getting on his nerves, if he was looking forward to finishing the project and getting rid of her son, but she was afraid he might say yes and yes.

She also wanted to ask what was going to be done with the structure when it was completed, seeing that she had no place to put it, but there never was a time when she saw him alone and she didn't want to ask in front of Dylan.

She finally had a chance one evening when she went to pick up Dylan at the ranch. After she admired their progress, her son went to wash the paint off his hands. She and Brandon were left alone as the shadow of the barn lengthened over the temporary construction site and the fading sunlight cast a golden glow over the house and the fields. She sighed. It was her favorite time of day. It *used* to be her favorite time of day.

Brandon leaned against the shed, crossed his arms over his chest and observed her without speaking. His blue chambray shirt was buttoned halfway, exposing his chest lightly dusted with dark hair. She had a wild desire to slide her hand inside his shirt, to run her palm over his chest. She shivered though the evening was balmy. Yes, she was getting more like Willa Mae every day. Desperate. And she hadn't even hit thirty yet. She swallowed hard and jerked her gaze away.

"I'm afraid I'm imposing on you, leaving Dylan here every day. I'm sure you had no idea this would happen when you volunteered to fix up the tree house," she said.

"That's right, I didn't," he admitted. "Or I never would have suggested it. But it hasn't been that bad."

Not that bad, she mused. Not good, but not that bad. At least he was honest.

"I assume you're almost finished," she said.

"We were, but then we decided to add shelves and paint it. Not just for looks, but for protection against the weather."

She nodded. *We* were. *We* decided... She couldn't believe an authoritative macho man like Brandon would let a child participate in the decisions. What a father he would have made if only...

"It's meant a lot to Dylan to have this project," she said. "It's been so good for him. You've been good for him. He doesn't talk about his father as much, at least not to me. I was hoping..."

"Don't get carried away with high hopes," Brandon warned. "You must know that's why he's here, that's why he's motivated. That's why he works so hard. Because this is where his dad is coming to get him. He's a very determined, stubborn kid. Like his mother."

"I don't know how to take that," she said, narrowing her eyes.

"Take it as a compliment," he said. "That's how I meant it."

"A compliment from you. A rare treasure. I'll remember it," she said lightly. She *would* remember it. Partly because it was a rarity. Partly because it came from him.

"You make me sound like an ogre," he said. "Am I that bad?"

"No, of course not. You've been more than decent about this whole thing. What I want to know is why? We know why Dylan hangs out here, what motivates him, but I don't know what motivates you. Why are you going to all this trouble?"

"I told you," he said. "I want the tree house repaired because it's dangerous."

"You could have hired someone to repair it. You didn't need to involve yourself or Dylan. You must have your own work to do."

"I do have work to do. But something happened when I got here. I thought it would be easy to concentrate out here with no distractions, but it isn't. I don't know what's wrong with me. In the past I've even been accused of being a workaholic." He grimaced at the memory, and Laura wondered who'd accused him of it. His wife? Or his associates, after his wife had died? He continued. "But now it's different. Maybe it's the distance, but I can't seem to get into my work the way I used to do. There are days when I sit out on your porch and just stare out at the scenery."

She wondered if he realized he'd said *your* porch. Would he ever feel at home here?

"It's much easier to pick up a hammer and nails and build something. So don't give me any credit for being nice to Dylan. He's given me the excuse I need not to do the work I don't want to do."

"But I thought he'd drive you crazy with his endless chatter and his questions." *And the fact that he'd remind you of the son you lost.*

"Sometimes he does. I came here for the solitude, you know. But I didn't realize how quiet it would be. No traffic, no sirens, no dogs barking, no car alarms going off in the middle of the night. At first I couldn't sleep, it was so quiet. Not that I miss the city. I don't. I'm just saying I haven't minded having him around as much as I thought I would."

Laura nodded. Another backhanded compliment. This time for Dylan.

"As soon as it's finished we're going to move it to wherever you live, you know. Dylan's not going to like it, but that's how it's going to be." He brushed the sawdust off his shorts with an air of finality.

Laura nodded. She knew only too well that was how it was going to be.

"Any luck finding a place for yourselves?" he asked.

"Not yet, but something will turn up," she said with more confidence than she felt. She was beginning to wonder if anything would turn up. "The whole town is focussed on the Fourth of July festivities right now, so it's a bad time to be househunting." She didn't say that any time was a bad time for looking for a rental in Silverado.

"So the Fourth of July is a big deal around here," he said.

"Oh, a very big deal. Wait till you see the parade. You are coming to the parade, aren't you? And the picnic and the fireworks?"

"I don't think so," he said.

"Oh." She couldn't keep the disappointment from hitting her like a large, leather sack of mail tossed off the back of a delivery truck. She didn't know why. She'd managed to enjoy the festivities in the past without him; she'd certainly be able to do so this year without any problem. But it might do Brandon some good to see the town enjoying simple pleasures. Who was she kidding? She wanted to see him. He intrigued her. He attracted her. She wondered how much of it was mutual.

"I'm not one for holidays," he explained.

"But this is a special holiday. Silverado was actually founded on the Fourth of July."

"What a coincidence," he said dryly.

"Not really. They did it on purpose. Which makes it easy to remember and gives us even more reason to celebrate. But if you don't like holidays..."

"I don't," he said.

"I see," she said.

Then it hit her. It was on the Fourth his family was killed. How insensitive she must seem. She didn't know what to say. Anything she'd say would be tactless or misconstrued as pity.

"It's not just a parade," she continued, trying to change the subject but not knowing how. Not knowing why she didn't just shut up and forget it. But she didn't. "And it's not just for kids. It's fun for everyone." As if that made any difference. As if that applied to him. She didn't know why she continued when the look on his face told her it was useless, that he'd already made up his mind and he wasn't going anywhere near a hokey small-town celebration and risk pain, but she did. "There's a picnic afterward and fireworks at night." The more she said, the worse she sounded. Like a one-person visitors' bureau or the chamber of commerce.

"Sounds good," he said. "I'm sure it's a lot of fun. But not for me." His tone was firm. She got the message. Leave him alone. He didn't want to get involved. Not with the town and not with her.

ON THE WAY HOME she went over their conversation in her mind. She hoped she hadn't come on too strong about the Fourth of July. Whether he came or not was completely immaterial to her. She also hoped she'd conveyed a sense of optimism about the future and not the dread she was experiencing every time she thought about her failure to get the job she'd wanted and even more important, to find a place to live.

She didn't want Brandon's pity any more than he wanted hers. That was one thing they had in common. One thing and not much else. Except for the fact that they'd both suffered losses. But he was rich, she was poor. She had a child to raise, and he didn't. He was a city person, trying to adjust to the solitude and the quiet. She was a country girl trying to get used to living in town. A small town, but still a town.

She glanced at Dylan and realized how lucky she was that he'd stopped complaining. About moving, about the tree house, about his aunt and anything else he could think of. For giving him something else to think about, something else to do everyday, she owed Brandon a huge debt of gratitude. She'd tried to thank him today, but she hadn't done a very good job of it. She'd try harder next time.

In the meantime she'd try to take her life one day at a time, instead of worrying about the future which loomed ahead like a brick wall she was speeding toward and would inevitably end up crashing into.

One morning when her aunt had had once again expressed her sympathy and incredulity at the Postal Service's failure to do the obvious and hire her niece, then left to do her grocery shopping, Laura took a call for a reservation for the Fourth of July weekend. As she flipped through her aunt's reservation's book, she noted there was only one room free, the one she and Dylan occupied. Taking a deep breath, she quoted the room rate and confirmed the reservation though it meant she and Dylan would have to move out for the weekend. She couldn't deprive her aunt of the chance to fill her B and B. Besides, they'd taken advantage of her hospitality long enough.

It was time to get serious about finding a place to stay, a place of their own. Now that she knew she wasn't going to get Willa Mae's place for sure. This was a wake-up call. The trouble was, Laura had asked around, she'd posted a notice on the bulletin board at the feed-and-fuel store but she'd heard nothing. It was such a small town, if there was a vacancy, she would have heard about it. She had to find a place for herself and Dylan now. But where and how?

What she'd told Brandon about the town being preoccupied with the celebration was true, but it wasn't the reason she hadn't found housing. The reason was there wasn't any. There were no apartments in town, only an occasional room for rent, and she was afraid that's where they'd end up, renting a room like some transient. It was too depressing to even contemplate. But right now it didn't look as if she had much of a choice.

In the mean time she was in charge of the historical society's entry in the Fourth of July parade. She called a meeting one evening at the old Victorian house that housed the historical society to try on costumes from the wardrobe in the attic.

"You look like Martha Washington," Aunt Emily declared when Laura came down the stairs from the attic and posed in a pink satin dress trimmed in white lace at the bodice and cuffs. "Just beautiful."

"Thank you, Aunt, but is it authentic? This dress was a donation and we have no idea of its origin. It may well be revolutionary, and Silverado was founded in 1852, not 1776."

"It could be revolutionary," David Ray cut in. "But it could also be authentic dance hall girl, the kind the gold diggers came to town to see." He held up an old archival photo of a girl in a long dress with a low-cut neckline and a nipped-in waist, like the dress she was wearing.

"The important thing is we girls get to look sexy one day of the year," Willa Mae said with a sly wink. "That's the whole idea."

"Not too sexy," her aunt cautioned, "or they'll take us for employees of the brothel."

"Let them take us," Willa Mae declared, dramatically waving a feather boa. "Do what you want, but I plan to make a splash and look as sexy as possible. And so should you, Laura. We get a lot of onlookers, a lot of tourists at our parade who don't know Martha

Washington from a dance hall girl. I say you should wear it and let the nitpickers be damned.''

Amanda, the town librarian, shook her head. ''I don't know what's gotten into you since you retired, Willa Mae. You used to be an upright pillar of the community. Now you're acting like you're in Reno already. That's not the way we dress in Silverado. But, then, I guess Silverado isn't good enough for you anymore. The lights just aren't bright enough.''

''You got that right, Amanda. Life doesn't end at sixty-five, you know. I've decided to have a little fun in my sunset years. Which is why I'm leaving this burg behind me and hitting the trail. You wouldn't believe the nightlife in Reno. And when I get tired of Reno—there's Las Vegas. Talk about bright lights. The place never shuts down.''

''The grass is always greener on the other side for some folks,'' Amanda muttered.

''Grass is for cows,'' Willa Mae said. ''I'm not looking for grass. I'm looking for excitement.''

Before tensions rose any further and erupted into a catfight, David grabbed a three-cornered hat from the trunk in the middle of the room and slapped it on his shaggy mane. ''What do you think of this?''

''You look like Napoleon at the battle of Waterloo.'' Willa Mae giggled.

''Napoleon had nothing to do with Silverado history.'' Amanda sniffed. ''We're a town of gold miners and merchants and ranchers.''

''Don't be such a stickler for details,'' Willa Mae said. ''Wear it, David. It brings out the conqueror in you.''

''Don't you mean emperor?'' Amanda asked.

David grinned and winked at Aunt Emily and she

smiled demurely at him. Laura followed this exchange with interest. Emily was positively glowing in her own antebellum gown. She wondered idly if her aunt was at all interested in the handsome, silver-haired newspaper editor. He was certainly an attractive man in her age bracket, who'd been editing their little newspaper for as long as she could remember. If her aunt was looking for someone, she could do a lot worse.

Laura always wondered if he really enjoyed writing about high school sports and the Elks Club's fund-raisers. She knew he was a fugitive from a big-city paper who'd tired of the fast pace and bad news. In Silverado, he'd found a place where he could accentuate the positive news. But as far as she knew, he'd never found a wife.

Laura took off her Martha Washington/dance-hall girl dress in the slope-roofed attic and hung it on the rack until the Fourth, then changed into her shorts and T-shirt. She had to get back and put Dylan to bed. But just as she reached the door of the once-grand mansion, she paused when she heard Brandon's name mentioned.

''I think he's quite an addition to the community,'' someone said. It sounded like Willa Mae.

''What's the story on him?''

''A hermit. A recluse.''

''Rich, good-looking. Too good to be true.''

''Do you know how much he paid for the ranch?''

''A lot. He's inflating real estate values, that's what it is. Why did she sell anyway?''

''Oh, come on, you know why.''

Quietly Laura closed the door behind her and walked out onto the street. She shouldn't be surprised that people started gossiping about her before she'd even left the building. She'd lived around here all her life. These people had known her all her life. Known her and cared about her and talked about her. There was nothing she could do to stop them from doing any of those things. Nothing she could do to stop the ache in her heart that such talk generated. She was just glad Brandon hadn't been there. He wouldn't have liked what he heard.

Instead of allowing herself to wallow in self-pity, she turned her thoughts back to Brandon as she walked back to her aunt's house. She wished he'd make more of an effort to get the know the locals. Not that it would stop the gossip he was generating. He was too handsome, too mysterious, too rich to simply ignore. But he'd have a chance to stop the rumors of his turning the ranch into a theme park or his hiding out from the law. On the other hand, he'd probably rather have people say things like that than know the truth. That he'd come to Silverado to mourn the loss of the family he loved. That he didn't want company and he didn't want new friends. And that included her.

Chapter Eight

The Fourth of July started out like any other summer day in that corner of Nevada. Hot and dry and dusty. But there was more than dust in the air. There was a palpable sense of excitement that hung over Silverado. As the sun rose over the majestic mountains in the east, the locals knew it wasn't just another day. In Silverado, the Fourth was more than the Fourth of July. More than a national holiday. It was also the anniversary of the arrival of the first settlers during the gold rush. Not just Laura, but many others in town could trace their family history over one hundred years back to that time.

In the town square a committee of three old codgers in overalls and wide-brimmed hats who'd been in charge of the barbecue forever was assembling the makeshift grills fashioned of fifty-five-gallon steel drums cut in half lengthwise with grates welded of rebar. Sheriff Patzert along with his three deputies were blocking the streets for the parade route, and some of the merchants like Danny at the feed-and-fuel were sweeping and hosing down their sidewalks. Naturally they'd close down at ten for the parade, but they'd reopen afterward.

Dylan jumped out of bed at dawn and packed his duffel bag to take to his friend's where he was spending the weekend. Very fortunately and even more conveniently, since this was the weekend he and Laura couldn't stay at the B and B. For once Dylan was talking about something other than the tree house or his daddy. Instead he was talking about his gold-digger costume, which consisted of coveralls and a bandanna around his neck and real cowboy boots. He was not only talking about it, he was wearing it, though the parade was hours away.

He clumped down the stairs to breakfast and fixed his own cereal. He sat in the breakfast nook and looked up at Laura who was helping her aunt prepare breakfast trays with fresh fruit, biscuits and homemade jam for the guests, to be delivered to their rooms.

"Is Brandon coming to the parade?" he asked.

"I don't think so," she said. "He's probably got something else to do. Like his work."

"On a holiday?" her aunt injected.

"For some people it's just another day," Laura said lightly, hoping they'd both drop the subject.

"Maybe he'll just come for the fireworks," Dylan said.

"Yes, maybe." She understood why Brandon didn't want to come. She didn't approve of it, but she understood. But no one else would unless they knew his whole story. And that wasn't going to happen.

Dylan took off, Laura and her aunt put a sprig of lavender on each tray and Laura delivered them to the guests. Then she picked up her small overnight bag she was taking to Willa Mae's, who'd offered her foldout bed in the living room when she heard Laura was stuck for a place to stay this weekend.

"This place should have rightly been yours," Willa Mae had said. "Everyone knows it. Everyone says it."

"Everyone but the district office," Laura said sadly.

"Honestly," her aunt said, taking note of the overnight bag, "I feel like a heel turning you out in the cold like this."

Laura kissed her cheek. "For one thing, it's hardly cold out there, and for another, we've intruded on you long enough."

"Nonsense. Say you'll be back for breakfast. Otherwise you'll starve. That Willa Mae never could boil water to save her soul. I can't stand to see you lose a single pound," Emily said giving Laura a critical glance. "And after the weekend, that room is yours, period. For as long as you want it. See how much good it's done Dylan to be here. Why, he's a different boy from the one who arrived a few weeks ago. Of course, part of that is due to Mr.... well, to the tree house project, don't you think?"

"I do think so," Laura said. "I'm just worried about what will happen when it's finished. They can't keep building shelves and painting boards forever. One of these days it will be finished and Brandon will ask where it goes. I've got to have a place to put it. And when I do put it somewhere, somewhere that isn't the ranch, Dylan's going to—I don't know what he's going to do."

She could only imagine the shock. All this time they'd been rebuilding, she had refrained from bringing up the subject of the change in location of the tree house. She didn't think Brandon had mentioned it, either.

"In any case," Laura said, "I'd love to come for breakfast. But I'm going on a campaign to find housing starting next week," she said resolutely. It was good to have a safe haven and someone who cared about her and Dylan. But she had to find a permanent home for the two of them. Enough was enough.

"You're starting your new job next week," her aunt protested. "Give yourself a little time."

A little time. If that was all she needed.... She needed a *lot* of time and a *lot* of money and a *lot* of luck. So far, she had none of those. She made a mental list of what she did have. Wheels. Maybe it was an old truck with worn-out brakes and an iffy water pump, but it ran. A job. Not the job she wanted, but a job, nonetheless. A son. A sweet, adorable little boy whose happiness and well-being was strictly in her hands.

BRANDON HAD TOLD himself he wouldn't go. Going to the Silverado Fourth of July celebration would just make him feel worse, if that was possible. He'd stay home and pretend it was just another day and not the anniversary of the accident. But by evening he could no longer pretend. He'd drive in and watch the fireworks from a safe distance and come right back. It would distract him for an hour or so. He would avoid seeing anyone he knew, in particular Laura or Dylan.

But he couldn't avoid Willa Mae, the outgoing postmistress. She spotted him across the lawn in the park at dusk before the fireworks began and hurried over to his side.

"Good to see you again." Wearing a jaunty straw hat with a red, white and blue ribbon and carrying an overnight bag, she smiled at him so eagerly that he was afraid she was going to insist on giving him that apricot cordial this time. But she didn't. "Have you seen Laura?" she asked.

He shook his head. He hadn't seen her and he had no intention of seeing her. "I just got here," he explained.

"Well, she's here somewhere. If you see her, would you give her a message for me? Tell her something's come up and I have to renege on my invitation to spend the night. You see, her aunt's booked up this weekend and Laura didn't have any place to stay, so of course I volunteered my foldaway in the living room, but my sister just popped into town unexpectedly—not the one who lives in Reno. This is my sister from California. Anyway, I've got to go. Here's Laura's bag."

She shoved it into his hand and skittered away into the darkness in her white running shoes before he could protest. He tried to tell her that he wasn't staying. That he'd just dropped by to see the fireworks, that he had no intention of running into Laura, but Willa Mae was gone. He could have pursued her and given her back the overnight bag, but he had no idea where she'd gone. So he didn't try. What good would it do?

He just stood there staring off into the gathering dusk, feeling a strange sense of destiny overtake him. He wondered if it mattered what he'd planned. Since he'd arrived in Silverado his life seemed to have taken a strange turn that he couldn't alter.

It was getting dark fast. There were voices all around him. One stood out. A child's voice.

"Brandon." It was Dylan. He came out of nowhere like a whirling dervish and flung himself at Brandon, wrapping his arms around his legs. "Thought you weren't coming. Save me, save me." For a moment Brandon was shocked and surprised. Was he in trouble? He must be. The boy had never shown any physical affection for him. Brandon reached down and put his hand on Dylan's head. His hair was like corn silk.

"What's wrong?" he asked.

What was wrong was that Dylan was being chased by two small boys, and all three were laughing their heads off.

"Ha, ha, you can't get me. Brandon won't let you." Dylan twisted around so he was behind Brandon, peering at his cohorts from between Brandon's legs. Using Brandon for a pole, they ran around him, chasing each other until they finally collapsed exhausted on the grass, chortling uproariously.

Brandon watched them, a smile playing on his lips, amazed at how little it took to send them off into hysterics. For once he didn't think of his own son, didn't wonder what it would be like if he were now eight years old, hiding behind his legs and tumbling on the ground. He only marvelled at the resilience of youth, of the joy and exuberance of children.

He felt absurdly flattered that Dylan would seek him out, him, a stranger in this big gathering in this small town, where presumably there were many old friends he could have approached. Which made him realize that he and Dylan were no longer strangers. Through the past weeks of working together on their project, they'd forged a bond. Just the thing he'd never wanted—a bond with a boy who was not his, never would be his. He couldn't afford to take any more losses.

He didn't want to form any attachments, not with women and certainly not with children. But somehow it had happened. At that moment, looking down at the boy wriggling on the grass, he had to admit he wasn't sorry it had happened. Besides being full of the same energy and determination that characterized Laura, Dylan was good company in his refreshing eight-year-old way. No pretensions, no hidden meanings behind his words, just forthright candor and honesty that amused and amazed Brandon.

"Where's your mom?" Brandon asked when the laughter and shrieks had finally subsided and the boys lay on the warm grass like little mummies.

Dylan jumped to his feet and waved his arm toward the bandstand. "Somewhere. I dunno. I'm spending the night with Jeremy." He pointed to one of the boys on the ground. "Cuz my aunt's full up this weekend."

"Yes, I heard." Brandon looked around. He had to find her. Had to give her the message and her bag.

"Are you okay, Dylan?" he asked the boy.

"'Course. Jeremy's mom is saving us a place for the fireworks." He paused and looked up at Brandon. "But my mom doesn't got anyone to sit with," he said with a pointed look at Brandon.

Brandon nodded. He didn't ask why his mom couldn't sit with him and his friend. It didn't matter because he decided there and then he wasn't going to stay for the fireworks. Stretched out on a blanket next to Laura under the stars with dazzling lights bursting overhead illuminating her face? Oh, no, not a chance. He wasn't made of stone.

The best thing for Laura was to find an eligible local man to marry. The best thing for him was to follow his original plan and isolate himself from women and children and the town itself. But despite this plan, he'd been sucked into their lives. He'd eaten dinner with her aunt, he'd been offered an apricot cordial by the postmistress, confided in by the newspaper editor, given advice by the garage mechanic and his son, and he thought about them, wondered about them, and yes, he even cared about them in some strange way he could never have anticipated.

Thinking, wondering and caring about the townspeople, that was okay. That was good. But falling for one of them, that was not good. That was disloyal. That was unfair and that was not possible. That was a path he couldn't take. He wouldn't—couldn't—ever love again. Because loving made you vulnerable. Loving exposed you to the most unimaginable losses. He looked up at the vast Nevada sky above him. Venus, the evening star, was just visible. It made him feel like there were larger things in the universe than his own concerns.

What was wrong with him, worrying about falling in love again? There was no possibility of that happening. Laura was a desirable woman, yes. And he enjoyed her company. Of course he did. So what was the harm in spending the Fourth of July with her? There wasn't any.

Chances were he'd never find her in this crowd anyway. But he'd try. And when or if he did, he'd hand her her overnight bag. If she insisted he stay, he would. Where would she spend the night? That wasn't his problem. She must have friends in town. Of course she did.

LAURA WRAPPED HER ARMS around her knees and gazed up at the sky. She missed Dylan, but she knew he was having the time of his life, running around with his friends. She couldn't bear to spoil his fun by demanding he sit with her for the fireworks. There were friends all around her. She was surrounded by people she'd known all her life, and yet she'd never felt so lonely, sitting there on a large handwoven blanket by herself.

Maybe it was because Dylan wasn't sitting next to her as he had for the past eight years of his life. It certainly wasn't because she missed her ex-husband. He'd missed the fireworks every year, saying he had better things to do. Maybe it was just her mood. Maybe it was because she lived in town now and her life had changed. Or maybe, just maybe, it was because Brandon wasn't there at the park. How could that be? How could she miss someone who wasn't part of her life and never had been?

Yet, when she saw him walking toward her in the dark, her heart started pounding so fast, and she pressed her hand against her chest. He'd come. He was there.

"Hi," he said. "Got any extra room?"

She nodded, unable to speak, and scooted to one corner of the blanket.

"Willa Mae asked me to bring you your bag," he said, dropping to the ground, bag in hand. "She said she's sorry, but she can't offer you a bed because her sister's in town."

She felt a sinking sensation somewhere behind her

ribs. No place to live. No place to stay. She found her voice at last, but all she could say was "Oh."

He turned toward her, his forehead creased in a frown. "Is that going to be a problem?"

She tore her gaze from his handsome face, touched by his concern, and tried for a casual tone to her voice. "No, of course not. No problem at all. I—I'll...find another place. See, my aunt is booked up for the weekend."

"So I heard," he said. "What time are the fireworks?"

"Nine o'clock."

There was a long silence. Fifteen minutes to go. She had no idea where she'd spend the night. Or what they'd talk about for the next quarter of an hour. She wanted to know why Brandon had come, what made him change his mind and if he was staying for the fireworks, but she couldn't ask, so instead she tilted her head and observed the stars.

"My father used to say that the fireworks were a waste of money. He thought the heavens provided a big enough show for anyone," she said.

"Is he still alive?"

"No," she said. "He died three years ago after a stroke. My mother followed him in death just as she did in life, and passed away soon after. All of dad's life he was an amateur astronomer. When I was small he'd drag me out to watch a meteor shower or just the evening sky, and he'd hand me the binoculars and tell me what I was seeing. Just as his father did with him."

"You're lucky," Brandon said. "To have a view like this. And a father like that. In the city there's always too much ambient light. So I had to make do by going to the planetarium for a view and an explanation of the heavens. To this day I can never remember the names of the constellations.''

''Well, that's the Big Dipper,'' she said.

''Give me a little credit,'' he said. ''I do know the Big Dipper.''

''What about Perseus?''

''Who?''

Impulsively she took his hand and pointed to a group of stars in the northern sky. ''That's him. He's the son of Zeus.''

He wrapped his hand around hers so securely he must have been able to feel her pulse speed up.

She forced herself to concentrate, though somehow he was now sitting so close, she could smell his hair and his clean shirt. ''In Greek mythology Perseus was tricked into going to find and bring back the head of the Medusa. He did it, but he never could have succeeded if Hermes hadn't given him a sword and if Athena hadn't given him a shield of polished brass.''

''Then what?'' he asked in a voice as dark and intimate as the sky.

Her mind was blank. Though she knew the story as well as she knew her name, she had no idea what happened next.

''He—he got the head. I don't remember how, but he did and then he came home. Oh, yes, and on the way, he rescued Andromeda who was chained to a rock and he later married her.''

''Sounds like quite a guy,'' Brandon said, his hand still wrapped around hers.

''He was. See, that's his leg and there's Medusa's head in his hand.''

"I hope you've told Dylan this story," he said.

"This one and many others, but I'm not sure he's as interested in them as I was. As you've noticed, he's got cars on his mind, not stars."

"I confess I was just like that at his age. I also confess I still like fast cars."

"So I noticed," she said dryly.

"Speaking of cars," he said.

"Let's not," she said lightly, fearing he'd start in again on the condition of her truck.

Just then a small red rocket went off in the sky and the crowd clapped loudly.

"Oh, good," she breathed, pulling her hand away from him. At last she could relax, look at the fireworks, stop talking and forget about Brandon. She stole a glance at his profile. Forget about Brandon? Who was she kidding? She could no more forget about him than forget about breathing. Especially when he was sitting next to her, leaning back on his elbows as the rockets burst overhead, the flares lighting his rugged features and the sound of ooohs and ahhhs filling the air.

Finally she leaned back and made her mind a blank, ooohing and ahhhing with the rest of the crowd. Forgetting to worry about where she was going to live, where she was going to spend the night and how she was going to spend the rest of her life. She let the warm summer air caress her skin and the illuminations fill her senses with their spectacular firey glow.

When it was over, she had to shake herself to return to reality. Brandon took her elbow and helped her up. The crowd swirled around her, but she was only aware of Brandon next to her, looking down at her, a mixture of concern and desire in his eyes. She was glad he kept his hand on her arm, because her legs were unsteady, as if she'd been sitting there for the past week instead of just a half hour.

"Come home with me," he said, his dark eyes fixed on her face.

"What?" She must have misunderstood. She couldn't go home with him. It wasn't her home.

"You have no place to go. I have a big house with many bedrooms, and many beds. You can have your choice. You've got your bag. Let's go."

She opened her mouth to protest, but no sound came out. She didn't know what to say. Spend the night at the ranch. It was unthinkable. But why? Why not spend the night there? It made perfect sense. There were a dozen reasons why she shouldn't, but for the moment she couldn't think of even one.

She was walking across the park, her arm brushing his, passing friends and acquaintances, murmuring greetings without knowing what she was saying. She was going to the ranch. She was going home. She was going home with Brandon.

His car was smooth and quiet and smelled like leather. They flew down the highway. So fast, she should have been scared. But she wasn't. She'd never felt safer in her life. Brandon was in control and she trusted him. She trusted him with her son and with her ranch and with herself. But did she trust herself? That was not a question she wanted to answer. Not now. Not tonight.

The house was dark. He parked in the driveway next to the night-blooming jasmine. They walked into the house, not touching, not speaking.

"See," he said as he opened the unlocked door, "I'm learning."

She smiled to herself. She was learning, too. To trust, to let go of her worries and fears. To live in the moment.

"Which room do you want?"

She hesitated, watching his face. Maybe it was a trick question. Because she didn't know what room he had. But the look in his eyes said this was no trick. The look in his eyes said he wanted her. That he was waiting for her answer.

She wavered back and forth in her leather-thonged sandals. But inside she was no longer wavering. She knew what she wanted.

"Yours," she whispered.

He nodded, a look of relief on his face so profound, she felt the breath whoosh out of her lungs. It was done. Decided. It was the Fourth of July. Independence Day. She was declaring her independence from Jason, from her job and her old life. Tomorrow she might be her old self again. But tonight she was a new and different Laura. He picked up her bag and started up the stairs. She followed him into the master bedroom. But the memories were too strong. Too wrong.

"No, mine," she said. "I moved back into my old room after my husband left."

They crossed the hall.

"It smells like you," he said, walking into the dark room with the flowered bedspread and the white curtains fluttering in the breeze and setting her bag on the floor. "Like you never left." His voice dropped to a whisper.

She held her breath. He crossed the room and

stood so close to her she could feel his warm breath on her cheek. But he didn't touch her.

''Maybe you never should have left,'' he muttered. Then he tilted her chin and gazed into her eyes, so long and so deeply, she felt as if she were drowning. Until their lips touched—then she knew she wouldn't drown. He would save her. At first it was only a light brush of his mouth against hers. Then he took control.

He kissed her like she'd never been kissed before. Like he'd been waiting all his life to kiss her, as she'd been waiting for him. So warm, so sure, so sensual. She wrapped her arms around him and hung on for dear life. Her body was heavy with long-forgotten desire. Her head was light and spinning. His kisses came faster and wilder and deeper. She joined him in this eternal dance of seduction until she no longer knew who was kissing whom. Whose tongue was entwined with whose, whose hands were gliding over whose back and whose hands were sliding up under whose shirt to caress the warm skin there.

All she knew was that she wanted him like she'd never wanted anyone. That if he didn't make love to her, she'd surely have to make love to him. Because the fireworks that were going off in her head outdid anything she'd seen tonight or ever.

As if he'd read her mind, his fingers were on the edge of her shirt, tugging it over her head and tossing it on the floor. He circled her nipples with his fingers through the lace until they peaked and she begged him to stop from the exquisite, unbearable ecstasy. He did stop. Just long enough so she could unhook her bra so her breasts could be free at last. And he could continue without the interference of the fabric.

He drew her toward the bed. He sat on the edge and pulled her onto his lap. He nuzzled the soft skin in the hollow of her throat while she pulled his shirt from his pants and unbuttoned it. She was breathing hard, desperate to feel his skin against her palms, to explore every inch of his body. How long had she felt this way? Since the first day she saw him in her driveway? Since he walked into the post office the first time? Since she saw him pounding nails without his shirt?

He was too impatient to let her fumble with those buttons. Instead he ripped the shirt off himself, then he set her back on her feet while he pulled his jeans off and left them on the floor. Next came his boxers. She gasped at the sight of him, so muscled, so broad-shouldered, lean and so obviously ready to love her.

Brandon reached for her then, unsnapped her shorts and oh, so gently removed them along with her lace bikini pants. He stood for a long moment and drank in the sight of her. She was so beautiful, more lovely than he'd imagined, her pale skin glowing in the light of the moon. All thoughts of other women gone. Every shred of guilt gone, too. His head was full of her. Her scent, her touch, her voice filled him and stopped him from thinking of anything and anyone but her.

He didn't know how they got to the bed. He just knew it was inevitable that they'd end up there together. What he didn't know was that she would straddle him and press hot eager kisses across his chest. That he would threaten to treat her the same if she didn't stop the delicious torture. But she continued until she'd covered his body with her soft lips, lingering along the way to take his manhood and drive him almost to disaster with her tongue.

He moaned and grabbed her arms. "My turn," he said between clenched teeth. He had her between his legs, stroking her tender skin on the inside of her thighs until she begged for mercy. Carefully, urgently, his fingers sought the most sensitive spot on her body. He stroked. She gasped. She shuddered and shattered into a million pieces, calling his name into the night air.

While she was still convulsing, he entered her with a deep, strong thrust. She was so hot, so tight, so willing and ready for him, he blew his chance to take it slow and easy. Again and again he entered her until he exploded. The air rang with his shouts. Utterly spent, he lay next to her, their hips joined, their naked bodies covered with a sheet he'd pulled over them.

Through the window he could see the stars and even the Big Dipper.

"He was right, you know," he murmured in her ear.

"Who?" she answered.

"Your father. The fireworks were a waste of money. It's better to make your own."

The smile on her lips as she drifted off to sleep made him feel like Perseus after he'd rescued Andromeda.

BUT THE NEXT DAY he felt like hell. Partly because she was gone when he woke up. Partly because his old demons came back to haunt him with a vengeance. What had he been thinking, bringing her back here, seducing her and not using protection? As if he'd have a condom or two lying around just in case...

He tried blaming it on the Fourth of July, his need to drown his sorrows or on the fireworks—or even on poor Willa Mae whom he suspected of plotting the whole thing. But it kept coming back to him. He'd invited her. He'd wanted her. Hell, he still wanted her. If he'd thought having her for one night would do it, he was badly mistaken. She wasn't that kind of woman and he wasn't that kind of man.

Neither one, he suspected, was into one-night stands. But that's all this was going to be. Because in his heart he'd promised Jeanne and he'd promised himself as well that their love was forever. The thought of deceiving her made him feel like he'd fallen into a black hole. What was he going to do now? How was he going to climb out of the hole? Apologize, for a start. Apologize to Laura. The sooner the better. He called her aunt's. Where else could she be?

"THERE, THAT OUGHT TO make you feel better," Aunt Emily said, pouring Laura a cup of herbal tea the next morning. "What happened? Did Willa Mae keep you up all night gabbing?"

Laura closed her eyes for a moment while she decided what to tell her aunt. "No, she didn't. As a matter of fact, she didn't have room for me after all."

Her aunt waited for a long moment. "So...?"

"So I had to find somewhere else to stay," Laura said.

"I see."

Laura sighed. What could she say? How could she

explain what she'd done without sounding like the fool she was? A one-night stand. That was what it was. That was all it was. No matter how wonderful it was, she knew and Brandon knew it would never happen again. By now he was most certainly racked with guilt. She didn't want to talk about it. She didn't want to face him. But sooner or later she'd have to do both. She might as well start now.

"I spent the night at the ranch," she said with a sigh. "I got a ride back this morning from Slim Baxter."

"I gather you're already having some regrets," her aunt said gently.

"No, but I'm sure Brandon is. He's told me in no uncertain terms that he'll never love again. I'm not the type to have an affair, Aunt. After what I've been through, I need stability in my life and in Dylan's life."

"So you're going to break it off?" her aunt asked, gazing at her from across the breakfast table.

"Fortunately or unfortunately, that won't be necessary," Laura said. "In his mind it's already broken off."

"You seem pretty sure of that," Emily said.

Laura nodded, stood and emptied her cup into the sink.

"Just a minute," her aunt said. "Aren't you going to try one of my cornmeal muffins?"

Laura shook her head. She knew she needed to eat but her stomach felt as if she'd ridden up an elevator in a high-rise and jerked to a stop on the seventy-eighth floor. "Thanks, anyway. They smell delicious. But I'm going to pick up Dylan and take him and his friends fishing at the trout farm." She had to get out and do something to erase the visions that danced in front of her eyes. Visions of Brandon in the moonlight, under the starry sky, with the rockets reflected in his eyes. His tenderness, his concern, the way he made her feel, like fireworks were going off in the room.

She had to pretend that nothing had happened. That her body didn't ache with longing to see him again. That it was an ordinary day after the Fourth of July. A holiday to be shared with her son before she started her new job.

"There are other men in the world," her aunt said kindly. "Other men who have no tragedy in their past."

"Who are looking to take on a divorcée and her son? I don't think so. From now on it's Dylan and me. I know I've said that before, but this time I mean it. I will not fall for any more handsome strangers who come to town and have no intention of staying the course. I thought I'd learned my lesson, but I hadn't." She shook her head and bit her lip to keep from crying. Not now. Not in front of her aunt.

"Aren't you being too hard on yourself?" her aunt asked, standing and putting an arm around her niece's shoulder. "He's an awfully nice man."

Laura nodded in agreement. He was an awfully nice man. Too nice. That was the problem.

"Where will you stay tonight?" her aunt asked, pushing her glasses up her nose.

"An old high school friend has offered me her spare room," Laura said. "You remember Brenda White? Unless she, too, has a last-minute visit from her sister, that's where I'll be. And if she does, I'll spread my sleeping bag in the town square before I'll go back to the ranch.''

Her aunt nodded slowly. Laura could tell she was worried and she wondered if she really should have burdened her aunt with her troubles. She managed a smile before she changed into shorts and left to pick up Dylan and his friend.

She heard her aunt's phone ringing just as she started her truck. She hesitated for a moment, then pulled out of the driveway. Why did she think it would be for her? Why did she hope it would be Brandon? She didn't want to talk to him. It was more likely someone calling to make a reservation.

Inside the kitchen her aunt answered, ''Silverado Inn.'' When Brandon asked for Laura, her aunt looked out the window to see the back of her truck disappear down the street.

''I'm sorry, she just left. May I take a message?'' she asked hopefully. She knew who it was. She also knew by the tone of his voice that he was just as upset as her niece and she wondered if Laura had correctly interpreted his real feelings. Emily had the distinct feeling that the man cared more than she realized, more than *he* realized, for Laura.

''Would you ask her to call Brandon?'' he asked.

''Of course.''

Brandon felt a ray of hope. He would talk to her. She would understand. They would be friends. Dylan would come back to work on the tree house. They'd find a permanent place to stay so he wouldn't feel like he'd stolen their ranch from them.

But she didn't call him back. She didn't call him that day or the next. He didn't see Dylan, either. He thought at least the boy would show up on his bike.

Not that he missed him. He had work to do, work that he'd been putting off while he worked on that tree house. He walked outside. The boards and the partially finished tree house stood outside the shed in the sun. Then he went back in the house and stared at his computer screen.

On Tuesday, Brandon could no longer take the solitude he thought he'd wanted, so he drove to town to pick up his mail at the post office. There was a strange man behind the counter wearing a regulation white shirt, blue pants and a tie. When Brandon asked for his mail, the man leaned across the counter and explained earnestly.

"We have a new system. Your mail is being delivered, starting today. Courtesy of the U.S. Postal Service."

Brandon almost pounded his forehead with his fist. He'd forgotten. If he'd just stayed at home, she would have driven by and left his mail, and he could have seen her then. Talked to her. Made things right. There was no way she could avoid him then. He glanced at his watch and turned around. If he raced back, he might still be in time to catch her on her route. But Willa Mae was blocking his way by standing there in the doorway.

"Did you find her?" she asked.

"Find her? No, she doesn't work here anymore. Oh, on the Fourth. Yes, I did. And I gave her her bag," he said, trying to edge around the former postmistress.

"And?" she said.

"And...she took it and found another place to stay. Everything worked out," he said. Sure it did. If you could call inviting her to her old house and seducing her "working out." "If you'll excuse me..." he said politely.

"Are you sure?" Willa Mae asked. "I was worried. After all, I invited her and then I had to let her down. Are you sure she found someplace to stay?" She wrinkled her forehead and peered up at him through her bifocals.

Brandon sighed. "I'm sure," he said, wishing she'd step out of the way. Hoping she wasn't going to insist on knowing *where.* Where had he found her a place to stay? Because he could just imagine the look on the old girl's face when she heard that she'd spent the night with him.

"She's a lovely girl," Willa Mae said.

"She certainly is," he agreed. He'd agree to anything if she'd just step aside and let him out of there.

"I'd give anything to see her happily married," she said, observing him through narrowed eyes.

"Yes, of course," he said. Then he paused. "To anyone special?"

"He'd have to be *very* special," she said.

Did she mean him, or did she mean he should step back so Laura could find someone special?

"If you folks wouldn't mind," the new postmaster called from behind the counter. "I believe you're blocking the entrance, which is strictly forbidden by Regulation Number 6590."

"I'm sorry," Brandon said over his shoulder. For once he was grateful for the postal service's bureaucracy. He had to get out of there before Willa Mae. "It was good to see you again, Ms. Willa Mae."

He felt her eyes on him as he sprinted to his car, and as he pulled away from the curb, she called to him, "Don't forget about that apricot cordial now, will you?"

Chapter Nine

Brandon broke the speed limit on the way back to his house. But he was too late. His mail was on his front porch in a sack on a wicker chair with a form letter asking him to erect a mailbox next to the driveway so the mail person wouldn't have to drive onto his property. He cursed under his breath, removed the mail and dumped it on the table, then sorted through the letters with ruthless efficiency. If it hadn't been for Willa Mae, he might have been there in time. But if it hadn't been for Willa Mae he might never have had that incredible night with Laura.

LAURA HAD PARKED off the road to eat her sandwich at noon when she saw Brandon's car whiz by in the direction of the ranch, at a speed of at least eighty miles per hour. Suddenly the bread and ham became a lump impossible to swallow or digest. She was just happy he hadn't seen the truck and that she'd missed him. She only hoped he'd get that mailbox erected by tomorrow so she wouldn't have to pull off and deliver the mail by hand.

But the next day there was still no mailbox anywhere to be seen. He hadn't been the only one. None of the other ranchers had complied with instructions, either. She'd had to drive onto their properties, honk her horn, wait for them to come out, and if they didn't, she'd had to get out of the truck and either hand them their mail in person or leave it in a conspicuous place. Which forced her to be behind her schedule by at least an hour.

By the time she'd reached his ranch, she was hot and irritable and frustrated. She pulled up in front of the ranch house and beeped her horn. When he didn't appear, she had to get out of her truck. Just as she'd done a dozen times that day with special delivery packages and registered letters and envelopes.

She walked up the steps to the front door, his letters and magazines under her arm, with a strange feeling of déjà vu. Well, what did she expect? It had been her house her whole life. She'd never be able to walk up those steps without feeling like she belonged there and he didn't. She knocked loudly, but there was no answer.

Somewhere in the background she heard water running. She followed the sound to the arbor and her herb garden. Brandon was standing there in wrinkled shorts, bare-chested and barefoot, watering her plants.

''Hello,'' she said loudly.

He spun around. ''Hello yourself.''

''Thank you,'' she said, glancing pointedly at the herbs.

''I couldn't let them die,'' he said, conveniently forgetting, she supposed, that he'd once threatened to pull them out and destroy the garden.

''As soon as I find a place to stay I'll come over and harvest them and dry them for winter. I appreciate your taking care of them until then. You didn't have to do that.''

''I know that. I'd be within my rights if I turned the hose on you,'' he said. ''After what you did to me.''

She thought back to that fateful day when Dylan climbed up into the tree house and refused to come down. The day when she sprayed Brandon with the hose and then laughed hysterically. Her mind raced. Is that what he meant? Or did he mean something else?

''Go ahead,'' she said. ''I deserve it. But you'd be soaking your important letters, too.'' She held up the mail in one hand to show him.

He ignored the letters in her hand; instead his gaze traveled over her body, his eyes lingering on her crisp white shirt, her waist and her legs. She stood there, trying to ignore this scrutiny and the threat of getting drenched in the middle of her route. But she felt the heat from his gaze. Just as if he'd caressed her here and there and everywhere. Like that night. Her knees wobbled. Her head felt as if it were floating above her body. She'd never fainted in her life, but she was afraid she might faint right there on the ground with his mail in her hand. Finally he turned the hose off and dropped it and she regained her equilibrium.

''What brings you by?'' he asked.

''Didn't you get my message?'' she asked. ''You're supposed to erect a mailbox.''

''Sorry, I've been busy,'' he said curtly.

She wondered what was keeping him so busy. He looked tired as if he hadn't slept for three days. She didn't want him to come any closer, but he did. He walked up to her, reached out and tilted her chin with the pad of his thumb to look into her eyes. She wanted more than anything to lean forward, to close the gap between them. But she'd learned. She'd really learned this time. Not to make a fool of herself.

"Look, Brandon," she said. "I can't deliver everyone's mail to their door. You have to get a mailbox."

"I know. I'll get one as soon as I can. I assume they have them at the hardware store."

"Yes. The specifications were in the letter I left for you and everyone else. You'd be amazed at how few people follow directions."

"Give me another day and I'll have the mailbox up. Look, can you come in the house for a minute? I'd like to talk to you."

"No. I'm behind schedule already," she said briskly.

"When can I see you?" he asked.

She wanted to say "Never." But she couldn't do it. Not with him standing there looking at her with those cloud-gray eyes, his lips so close, he could kiss her if he leaned forward just another few inches. The memories came flooding back. She promised herself she'd never step into that house again. On the other hand, they had to talk sooner or later. It might as well be sooner.

"We can talk right here," she said. "But I only have a few minutes."

He pressed his lips together in a straight line. Clearly this wasn't what he'd had in mind, but he had to accept it.

"You walked out on me," he said, his eyes hard as flint.

"I'm sorry. I was in a hurry. I didn't have time to thank you for your hospitality."

"Is that what you call it?" he asked incredulously.

She could feel her face turn scarlet.

"I don't want a thank you. I want an explanation," he said. "After a night like that, you ran away without a word. Without even a note."

"All right, here it is. I felt bad about what happened. I never should have accepted your offer and I never should have done what I did...." She couldn't bear to say *make love with you.* Because there was no love involved. At least not on his part.

"So you left," he said brusquely.

"What was the point in staying? Don't tell me you didn't feel just as bad as I did. Don't tell me you weren't feeling regret and guilt and God knows what else that morning?"

He couldn't deny it. He didn't deny it. Instead he reached for her free hand and took it between his. "You're right," he said gruffly. "That's how I felt. At first. But now...I miss you. I miss Dylan. Where is he?"

She couldn't help it. If he wanted to melt her resistance, he couldn't have done it better than by asking about her son.

"He's at day camp this week," she said with a half smile. "He agreed to go only because his friends were going. He'll be back here next week. If you want him, that is." She wrenched her hand from his and glanced at her watch.

"Of course I do. Wait a minute. Don't leave," he said. "Not until I've finished. In case I don't get another chance to tell you. That night with you... I'll never forget it. Never. It was incredible."

She clutched his mail to her chest and felt the tears sting her eyelids. She couldn't speak. Couldn't tell him anything. What the night had meant to her. The way he'd made her feel. It was just as well. Better to keep it bottled up inside. Forever. It was over. She felt relief, sadness, but no regret. She knew if she had the chance, she'd do it all over again. Just because she'd never made love to anyone like that. Never given herself, never gotten back more than she'd given.

"Here," she said, holding out his letters. "I've got to go now."

She marched back to her van in the driveway. Before she blurted out something else. Something she'd regret. She didn't look back. Not until she got to her official vehicle in the driveway. Then she sneaked a look in the rearview mirror and saw him standing there staring at her truck.

True to his word, he had a mailbox erected the next day when she drove by in her mail van. When she saw it, her heart fell. Yes, she wanted him to have a mailbox. Yes, she'd left him a note, and told him in person. Of course she didn't want to have to drive in there, see him again, be forced to engage in idle or awkward conversation. Then why the wave of disappointment she tried to stifle as she stuffed the shiny new box, with his name stencilled on the side in black letters. Could it be that she liked seeing him, hoped he'd take her hand, touch her face? Was it so wrong to enjoy talking to him and to imagine that he liked seeing her, too? If she did, it would be foolish in the extreme.

She didn't see him all week. Every day she glanced down the driveway as she delivered the mail to his box, but she never saw him. She wondered how often he watered her herb garden, but she didn't dare drive in to take a look. She didn't linger, or hand-deliver any special-delivery letters. By Friday she realized that was the way it was going to be. Which was exactly the way she wanted it.

When she picked up Dylan from day camp he had a whistle hanging around his neck from a lanyard he'd made out of leather scraps. He showed her a paper plate mask he'd decorated to look like a tiger, talked about playing goalie in the soccer game and said he wanted to go back to camp the next week.

She shouldn't have been surprised, since he seemed happy all week, but she was. Surprised and pleased. This was the same boy who'd scoffed at kids who went to day camp. Said they were babies and sissies. Now they were his friends.

"That's great. Then I don't have to worry about you, about what you're doing when I'm at work."

"Did you worry about me when I was at the ranch working on my tree house?" he asked.

"Well, no, not exactly. But..." What could she say? *Yes, I worried, but not for the reasons you think. Brandon didn't want you there. It isn't our home anymore. I was afraid you'd get attached—to Brandon and to the ranch. I wanted to avoid Brandon because I, too, was afraid of getting attached. That I'd make another awful mistake.*

Suddenly he slid down in his seat, his shoulders hunched up so he looked like the pet turtle he'd had when he'd been about five years old. Her spirits fell. What now?

"I'm not going back to the ranch," Dylan said in

a soft voice she could barely hear. "I'm never going back to my tree house."

"You're not?"

"No, cuz you know what?" he said. "My daddy's not coming back to get me."

She sat very still, without moving, slanting a glance at his face, looking for tears, her heart splintering in a thousand pieces. He'd finally said the words she'd waited to hear, wanted to hear, but now that he'd said them, she felt sick. She'd been hoping he'd grow up enough to accept his father's leaving them, but it was too soon, he was too young to have to face such a disappointment. His words were matter-of-fact, but his mouth was twisted into a grimace and one lone tear trickled down his cheek.

"Oh, Dylan," she said, and put her arms around him.

"He isn't, is he?" he asked, his voice muffled against her shoulder.

"No, he isn't."

"That's what I thought," he said.

"But you and I—we have each other. We always will. We're a family, you know, the two of us." She hugged him tightly.

He nodded. But his body was stiff. "Other kids have a dad and a mom," he said. She blinked rapidly. She couldn't let him see her cry. She couldn't. She didn't know what to say. She was filled with unspeakable regret and sadness. She buried her face in his hair.

After a long moment he pulled away from her. His eyes were dry, and his mouth was set resolutely in a straight line, his lips clamped together. In those few moments she felt he'd grown up. Too fast. Maybe it was selfish, but she wanted her baby back. She didn't know what else to say to him, so she didn't say anything. She thought of Brandon, remembered him saying *I miss you. I miss Dylan.* If he meant it, he'd be disappointed. If he didn't mean it, he'd be relieved.

Surely the latter was true. He'd be glad he could put away the saw and hammers and boards and get back to his own work. Wouldn't he?

DURING THE WEEKEND she stayed close to Dylan. As close as he'd let her. She suggested renting a movie to watch on her aunt's VCR. He shook his head. She mentioned swimming at the high school pool. He said no. Instead he sat on the front steps shuffling his baseball cards in his hands. She realized he was still processing the painful truth about his father. She was not going to be able to make up for the loss of his father, no matter what she did.

"What about taking your metal detector and going up into the mountain to look for silver?"

He shrugged. "Okay." He stood up. "We better ask Brandon to come."

"Brandon?" she asked, startled.

"Yeah, he wants to go up there. But he doesn't know the way. I told him I'd show him where your great-grandpa found the silver."

"Yes, but I don't think today is the day—"

"I'll call and ask him," Dylan said, ignoring her feeble protest.

She didn't have the heart to say no. Not when she'd finally interested her son in something. But Brandon could and would say no. She knew he would. He didn't want to spend any more time with her and Dylan any more than she wanted him to. So she got out the number and stood in the hall, just out of sight, but not out of hearing while Dylan picked up the phone. She shamelessly eavesdropped while he talked to Brandon.

"You wanna come up to the mountains and look for silver with us?" he asked.

A pause.

"Yeah. Uh-huh. 'Kay. All right." Then he hung up.

"He'll be here in a half hour," Dylan said matter-of-factly. He'd never doubted it. "Are we taking a picnic?"

Her aunt came around the corner from the kitchen. "Did I hear someone say picnic?" she asked.

"Yes, Aunt Em. We're going up into the mountain behind the ranch. Won't you come with us?" Laura asked. *Please come with us. Don't leave me alone with Brandon.* The more the merrier. There was safety in numbers, and so forth.

"Oh, no, I can't possibly. I'm working on my new ad for the newspaper. David is coming by to help me lay it out. I'm thinking of going color. David thinks it will make a big difference."

Laura nodded. Only half-aware of the way her aunt's eyes sparkled at the mention of the newspaper editor's name. Laura's mind was still spinning with thoughts of spending the day with Brandon and Dylan. Just when she thought they'd broken the connection completely—now that Dylan was no longer interested in the tree house, she'd thought she could pretend Brandon was just another post office customer—now this. She didn't have the heart to say no to Dylan. Not now. She was glad Dylan wanted to go anywhere with her.

She just wished she'd had some excuse for squelching his plan of inviting Brandon along. Now Brandon would think she'd put him up to it. That she really wanted to continue their relationship or, or...something. She shook her head and went to the kitchen. It was too late to worry about what he thought. He was coming with them. And Dylan was happy about it. That was all that mattered.

They were standing in front of her aunt's Victorian when he arrived. He was wearing khaki shorts and a polo shirt, his bare feet in deck shoes. Her aunt beamed at him. Laura took a deep breath and tried to keep her eyes off his broad shoulders and muscular legs.

"We should have come by to get you," she said. "The place we're going is on the other side of the ranch."

"That's all right. I'm driving."

She told him his car would never make it up the dirt road. He said it would, and against her better judgement they loaded a shovel and bucket, Dylan's metal detector and the picnic basket into his trunk.

She sat next to Brandon in the front seat. Dylan sat in back, leaning forward in his seat belt, talking incessantly about what he was going to do with the money he'd make from the silver he'd find. Brandon steered with one hand and rested the other arm on the back of her seat. His hand grazed Laura's shoulder when he turned the wheel. She was intensely aware of his touch. She fought off the memory of his hands on her feverish skin that night. That magic night she couldn't forget.

Dylan asked Brandon what he'd do with his share of the silver money.

''Maybe buy a small plane,'' Brandon said.

''A plane?'' Dylan's eyes almost popped out of his head. ''Can you fly a plane?''

''Yes. But I haven't been up for a while. I'd have to take some more lessons before I fly again.''

''Can I come up with you?'' he asked.

Laura slid a glance in Brandon's direction and she silently shook her head. She didn't want Dylan to be making plans to do things with Brandon. Things that would never happen. Dreams that would never come true. He'd had enough disappointment to last a lifetime.

''I don't know, maybe I'll get a sailboat instead,'' Brandon said.

''Where will you sail it?'' Dylan asked.

''Where's the nearest lake?'' Brandon asked.

While Laura gave directions, they talked about sailing and fishing and flying and hunting and all kinds of other activities that men and boys like. She didn't want to put a damper on their enthusiasm but she didn't want to encourage their plans, either, for the obvious reasons. Brandon had no idea how seriously children took this kind of talk. How much they counted on promises made. How much it hurt when promises were broken. But she didn't say anything.

They headed up the narrow dirt road, his car surging over rocks and potholes, his tires spinning on gravel. Every time his car hit a rock, they lurched forward and their seat belts tightened; she shot him a look that said she should have taken her truck.

He cheerfully ignored these looks and turned onto a small dead-end shale road to the site her grandfather used to take them and regale them with the story of his father's discovery. The mine shaft was long since closed, and the road was barely passable, but it was a breathtaking spot on the edge of a small stream, overlooking the valley and the town.

"That's it, isn't it Mom?" Dylan asked, hopping out of the car and pointing to a pile of rocks, some rusty tin cans and an old pump. "That's where your great-grandpa struck it rich."

She smiled. The ranch might be gone. Her parents were dead and buried. But as long as there were memories, the past lived on. Dylan would always remember the story of Great-Grandpa and the lost mule and some day he'd tell his children and they'd tell theirs and...

"Yes, that's it."

Dylan grabbed his metal detector and went off to look for treasure at the entrance to the old mine. Brandon stood on a rock and surveyed the scene below with his binoculars. "This is beautiful," he said. "Thanks for inviting me."

When she didn't say anything, he turned to look at her. "That's right. You didn't invite me, did you?"

"It was Dylan's idea," she admitted.

"I'm flattered," he said. "I really wasn't sure how he felt about me. Except that I was a threat. So when he asked me along today, I was surprised. And pleased. He's a good kid. But you know that."

"Not always," she admitted. "We've had our moments, he and I. But he's changed this summer. He was not a happy camper when I took him away from his home and his tree house."

"I don't blame him," Brandon said. "I should have been more understanding when he came back to the ranch. But I saw him as a threat, too. A threat to the solitude I craved. It's funny, but I've missed him this week. I have no more excuses to ignore my work, to go outside and saw some boards, get some exercise. When is this day camp over? When is he coming back?''

''He's not coming back to the ranch,'' she said, snapping a dried cattail in half. ''He's finally realized his daddy isn't coming back.'' She turned her face to the sun and closed her eyes so he couldn't see the tears that threatened to flow. ''So what's the point of building a tree house if your dad isn't coming to get you and you have no place to move it to?'' She hated the way her voice shook, afraid he'd think she was feeling sorry for herself, when it was her son she pitied.

''I see what you mean,'' Brandon said matter-of-factly, as if he hadn't noticed her voice was faltering. ''But that's what you wanted, wasn't it, for him to face the facts?''

''Of course. It was bound to happen sooner or later. It's just... Before, he had hope. He was working for something. He was excited. Working with you to finish the tree house. Waiting for his dad. Now, he's made a grown-up decision, but he's not grown up. He shouldn't have to be. Not yet. Not at his age. And it's my fault.''

''Your fault? What about your ex-husband?''

''It's too easy to blame him. Because he's the one who left, he's not coming back and he ran through all my money. But it takes two to make a divorce, so...what can I say? I must be partly at fault. But no one who had a perfect marriage could understand that.''

"I don't think anyone has a perfect marriage," he said slowly.

She turned her head in his direction. He was still looking through his binoculars, one hand braced on a granite boulder. She sat on the hard ground and leaned back against a sun-warmed rock, not knowing what to say. Afraid to say anything, afraid to move for fear he'd clam up. Just when he might be ready to talk about himself.

"Except me," he said.

She sighed. She should have known. "You're very lucky. I hope you know that."

He shot her an incredulous look. "Lucky?"

"No, no, I'm sorry. I didn't mean that. I just meant—"

"I know what you meant," he said, cutting her off. "I asked for it. Of course, it wasn't perfect. As much as I want to believe it was. We had our fights. I've just refused to remember them. She was headstrong, stubborn, opinionated and temperamental. I was stubborn, too. Still am. I told her not to go out that day. The streets were slick. She laughed at my fears. Said I was overly protective. If I'd only insisted. I should have taken her keys away from her. So you see, I'm to blame, too."

She shook her head. "I don't see it that way."

Laura was afraid to ask any more about his wife, but she realized it might be her only chance. She took a deep breath. "How did you meet?"

He set his binoculars down, sat down next to her and gazed out over the valley. There was a long silence. Either he was thinking of a way to end the conversation, change the subject or open up and tell her more. She could almost feel the struggle going on. Finally the latter option won.

''She was my college roommate's sister,'' he said at last. ''She came to visit one weekend and I was completely smitten. She was poised, self-assured with ferocious red hair. I should have known then she'd have an iron will and a temper to match. But I fell like a ton of bricks. We got married right out of college. Everyone said we were too young. That we'd change.

''We did change, but we also grew up together. I worked hard and so did she. We were sensible. We saved our money until we had a nest egg, bought a house, then when I cashed in my stock options, we decided it was time to have a baby. We'd waited a long time to have Stephen, so when he came—well, you know how it is, you pin all your hopes and dreams on that little being and then—'' He broke off.

She nodded mutely. Wishing she could offer some kind of comfort. But words were not enough. Impulsively she reached for his hand and squeezed it. Not knowing if he'd accept comfort, whether words or gestures. She held her breath. He didn't pull away. He turned to look at her. Their glances locked and held for a long moment. The mountain air full of the scent of wild herbs and pine needles heated up by several degrees.

Her pulse sped up so rapidly she was sure he'd notice. What had been sympathy turned to white-hot desire. He tightened his grip on her hand. Then he moved closer, or did she? The gap between them disappeared. His face blurred as he brushed his thumb across her lips. She was amazed at the shiver of anticipation, at the rush of emotion that shook her. She wanted more, but did he?

A cloud crossed the sun and a rock tumbled down from the hills above them and landed some ten yards away. They jumped to their feet. Was that the gods speaking? Telling her she was asking for more than she had a right to? That she was getting her hopes up for nothing? Informing her of what she already knew—that Brandon was a one-woman man?

"That was close," he said, turning to look up. He brushed his hands together briskly. "That must have been a sign. I've talked way too much about myself. I must be boring you to death. Even the sun's gone behind a cloud."

He looked relieved at the interruption. A sinking feeling of disappointment filled her chest. "I'm not at all bored," she insisted. "I'm flattered that you told me. It must be hard to talk about."

"Yes. It is. Or it was. You're a good listener. I always assumed no one would want to hear about it. It's not a happy story, after all."

"No, but the story isn't over, not yet. You have your life ahead of you."

He frowned.

"Sorry, I guess that's one of those clichés you've heard before," she said. "But it's true."

"You, too," he countered. "You've got your whole life ahead of you. Hasn't anyone ever told you that?"

She nodded. "My aunt told me just the other day. I had the same reaction you just did. But I know she's right. She always is."

"How's your new job?" he asked.

"Fine. I like being outdoors. I miss some of the

regulars who come into the post office every day, but I've seen some folks who live in the country, whom I don't usually run into. The only drawback is the lack of housing."

"You still haven't found a place?"

"We're still at my aunt's. She's incredibly gracious, but we can't stay forever."

He looked into his binoculars again. "All those houses down there, and no place for you?"

Their ranch—no, *his ranch*—was spread out below them like a Grandma Moses primitive painting, the dry riverbed, the barn and the sprawling ranch house and the acres of land surrounding it. Was he thinking what she was thinking? *It's so big. So big for one person.*

No place for you. The words echoed in the stillness of the air. She shivered. Without the sun on the mountain, the air was cooling off quickly. The faint sound of thunder rumbled in the distance.

Before she could think of an answer, Dylan came running from behind a boulder. "Look," he yelled, holding a gray rock streaked with silver in his hand. "Look what I found."

They pored over it, Brandon rubbing his thumb over the smooth surface then giving it to Laura to look at while Dylan jumped up and down excitedly.

"Is it valuable? Is it?" he asked. "Is it silver?"

"I don't think so," Laura said. "But it's beautiful anyway."

"It could be silver," Dylan said, taking the rock back. "If it is, we'll be rich as Great-Grandpa. Then we can get our ranch back."

Laura sighed. Just when she thought he'd accepted their fate, he came up with something like that. Brandon was staring at Dylan, the lines in his forehead deepening.

"Time for lunch," she said brightly, heading for the car where the picnic basket was still in the trunk. But the dark cloud overhead sent a few light drops falling on her head. Brandon took the basket from her.

"Rain, in the summer?" he asked, squinting at the sky. "I thought it never happened."

"It does up here. You can see it's still sunny down below. At the ranch and all over the valley. But as the warm air rises from the valley, it expands and the temperature drops. As you know, colder air can't hold the moisture, so it condenses out as rain." She held her arms out, tilted her head up and let the drops fall on her face.

He smiled. "Pretty impressive, Professor. Where did you learn so much about physics?"

She shrugged. "From my dad. A rancher has to be a weather forecaster, too. He used to study the skies, praying for rain up here, because the mountain streams fill our reservoir. I mean *your* reservoir."

"So what's the forecast?" he asked. "Do we stay and have our picnic?"

She studied the sky. She had no idea what would happen next. She didn't have the gifts her father had. The gray cloud could move on in minutes. Or it could turn black and the heavens could open up. It wasn't likely, but it could happen. She didn't know that much about weather. She had to admit she'd been showing off for Brandon. That she wanted him to think she was not as naive and stupid as she was sure she'd first appeared. And she didn't want to cut the day short.

"Let's give it a try," she said, spreading the red-and-white checkered tablecloth on the ground. "A little rain won't hurt us or our ham sandwiches."

Besides the sandwiches, Aunt Emily had insisted they take artichokes with hollandaise sauce left over from last night's dinner, three slices of cheesecake with raspberry purée, bottled water and a half liter of red wine.

"This isn't a picnic, this is a feast," Brandon said, sitting across from Laura.

"We can thank Aunt Emily for that. Aunt Emily and *The Great Cooks of the World* that she watches every day on cable TV."

Dylan was too excited to sit down. He turned his nose up at the artichokes, grabbed a sandwich and went back to look for more silver.

The sun came out again and Laura felt the warmth seep into her bones. Her eyelids were heavy and she yawned and leaned back on her elbows.

"I'll pack up," Brandon said, noting her lassitude. "You take it easy." After one glass of wine and an emotional spilling of his guts to Laura, he felt like taking it easy himself. What he really felt like was making love to Laura on the ground in the pine-scented air. Her sympathy, her quiet understanding, the warmth of her lips, the promise in dark eyes, or one he just imagined, were driving him crazy.

He told himself not to confuse sympathy and understanding with desire. He didn't know if she felt the same about him. All he knew was she was a warm, giving and very sexy woman, whether she was wearing a uniform or shorts and a formfitting T-shirt.

He packed up the basket and took it to the car. When he came back, she was lying on her side, with her chin propped in her hand. Her eyes were closed and she was breathing softly.

He sat down, wrapped his arms around his knees and watched her breasts rise and fall under her soft cotton T-shirt. He was hit by a sudden shaft of intense desire. What was wrong with him? Just because he'd unburdened his mind didn't mean he was free of his obligation to the memory of his wife and child. He had no right to lust after Laura. Oh, all right, he could lust after her, be unfaithful in his mind, as long as he didn't act on his feelings. Like the last time. But that's just what he wanted to do. He wanted to take her back to the ranch and make love to her. To spend another night with her and to wake up in the morning and find her still there.

He wondered offhandedly if he'd ever get tired of her—of talking to her, listening to her or of making love to her. He couldn't imagine ever getting his fill. But that didn't make it right. When Dylan appeared in the clearing, Brandon jumped to his feet, grateful for the interruption, pointed to Laura and motioned for him to be quiet. Then he went off with the boy to look for silver. But they didn't find any more treasure. The silver had been mined out long ago.

"But don't give up," he told Dylan. "Sometimes you find treasure where you least expect it."

As Laura lay there half-asleep, his words rang in the mountain air.

And she thought about them for a long time afterward. She'd never found any treasure. She wasn't looking for it. She wasn't expecting it. She suspected the McIntyre luck had run out with Great-Grandpa.

Chapter Ten

Summer faded into fall. Dylan went back to school, or Brandon assumed he did. True to his word, he never came back to the ranch to finish the tree house. Reluctantly Brandon went out to look up in the tree one day at the half-finished structure and knew he had to complete the work—Dylan or no Dylan. If he couldn't bring closure to the events of his own past, he could at least finish the tree house. Some day, some child would climb up there and wait for his daddy. A daddy that would be there for him and who wouldn't let him down.

Brandon set up his sawhorse once again and worked steadily in the autumn sunshine, ignoring his real work, putting off phone calls and leaving e-mail unanswered until he had completed a solid foundation. Four sides, a deck and a roof with overhanging eaves. He was proud of the way it turned out. He wished Dylan were there to see it, because if it hadn't been for Dylan, he would have torn it down. And that would have been a shame. He wasn't proud of himself for the way he'd reacted to the boy's appearance in the tree. The man who threatened to have the house torn down was a stranger to him now.

Maybe one day Dylan would even come back to visit.

Brandon climbed the new sturdy ladder he'd bought at the hardware store and sat on the small deck in the midst of the branches and looked around. It was a wonderful feeling being hidden in the leaves high above the ground. It made him feel young again. It was the kind of tree house he would have wanted as a child. The kind he would have built for his own son. Or for Dylan, if Dylan hadn't given up on his father coming back. He built this one because he had to. Because something inside him told him he wouldn't be at peace until he'd done it. Peace. It was so elusive. Sometimes he felt it. Sometimes he didn't.

He put his hand against the rough bark of the tree and noticed an indentation where squirrels had hidden acorns. There, inside, was a small scrap of paper. He pulled it out. It was Dylan's note to his father. He felt like a snoop, but he read it anyway.

> Dad. I miss you. Wen are you comeing bak? I'm lonly alone and lonesum. We had a move to town. Ill be wating for you there. Com and git me.
> your son, Dylan

Brandon held the note for a long time, smoothing it absently with his thumb. He felt his eyes burn with unshed tears. Tears for Dylan whose dad had deserted him. Tears for the family who had to give up their home. Tears for himself who'd been left without a son. Tears for the unfairness of life.

He turned the paper over, took a pen from his shirt pocket and wrote.

> Dylan, I miss you. Please come back. I miss you. If I had a son, I would want him to be just like you.
> Brandon.

As he wrote the words, he knew they were true. Dylan was everything a man could want in a son. Gutsy, tough and sensitive. He meant it when he said he missed Dylan. He never thought he'd say it or mean it, but he did. He missed his constant questions. He missed Dylan's enthusiasm and excitement when he got a new video game Brandon had to evaluate for a client. He'd had Dylan do the evaluating. It was made for kids, after all. He missed working with the kid on the tree house. He looked back on those days with nostalgia. He wondered what Dylan would think if he ever came back and read the note? What would he say if he saw the finished tree house? Was it the way he'd pictured it?

He missed Laura, too. More than he wanted to. After the picnic, he only saw her on the road where she gave him a casual wave from the post office vehicle. He hoped he'd receive a package too big for the mailbox, or a certified letter so she'd have to stop and get his signature, but it didn't happen. What he did receive, however, was an invitation to a farewell party for Willa Mae. He was surprised to hear she hadn't moved out of her place yet and he wondered where the new postmaster was living.

Even more important, he wondered where Laura and Dylan were living. He had a constant nagging guilty feeling every time he thought of them crowded into a single room at her aunt's when he had thirty-four-hundred square feet of ranch house to himself. The empty bedrooms, the unused dining room, the empty barn and outbuildings all echoed their reproaches when he passed by.

Where have they gone? they seemed to ask. *Who are you?*

He wasn't the party type, but he had to admit he was looking forward to Willa Mae's. He'd finally get a chance to see Laura again. He parked in front of the post office along with everyone else in town that Saturday evening and climbed the stairs around the back to the small apartment that had been cleared of Willa Mae's furniture and was now wall-to-wall people.

His hostess greeted him with an air kiss and a glass of punch. She was dressed in wide purple palazzo pants and a black turtleneck sweater. Her hair was streaked with bright orange. When she saw his gaze travel to her colorful hair, she grinned.

"It's the new me. Do you like it?"

"Stunning," he said. He meant it. He was stunned.

"Everyone's here," she said with a wink. "Including me. I was supposed to leave last month, but one thing after another. You know how it is. What is it they say? Forgotten, but not gone."

She waved him into the crowded apartment. His eyes searched the crowd. She had to be there. She had to. But she wasn't. Her aunt was in a corner talking to David Ray, the newspaper editor. They appeared so engrossed in each other, he hated to interrupt, but he did.

"I thought I'd see Laura here," he said after he'd dispensed with the minimum of small talk.

Her aunt glanced around the room as if for the first time, then drew her eyebrows together in a frown. "I know she was planning to come."

"Is she still living with you?" he asked.

Her aunt looked surprised he didn't know. "Oh, no, she's renting a place outside town. On the old Fleming place. I thought you knew."

"Where is it? Maybe I ought to go see if she needs a ride."

They gave him directions and he left the party and headed west on the highway. About three miles from town he saw her truck with the hood up, and nobody in it. Logic told him she was standing next to it on the shoulder, that something happened to her truck, but she was fine. But his heart banged against his ribs and there was a loud ringing in his ears. What if someone had come along...? What if she'd tried to cross the highway and a truck came along and...? If anything happened to her... He couldn't stand to lose anyone else he loved.

Loved? He didn't love Laura. He couldn't. He'd been blessed once in his life with a love so strong, so beautiful, that nothing and no one could ever match it. But sometimes he saw his life stretch ahead of him as lonely and empty as the highway that crossed the state. He pictured himself driving down that highway, the highway of life, his engine opened at full throttle, exceeding the speed limit, searching for something to fill the empty hours, days and years.

He swerved his car and parked it facing her truck, and jumped out.

"Laura," he shouted, his mouth as dry as the dust that covered the fields on either side of the road.

"Back here." She came around the back of her truck, her face streaked with dirt, her hair an untidy mess of curls. "Brandon, what are you...?"

The relief he felt almost overwhelmed him. He couldn't help it. He grabbed her and hugged her tight. At first tense in his arms, her body slowly relaxed and she clung to him.

"I knew someone would come," she said, her voice shaky. "I didn't know when or who."

He held her at arm's length and looked into her eyes. Those glorious amber eyes that regarded him with a mixture of relief and gratitude and something else. Something he dared not think was anything deeper.

"What in the hell happened?" he asked. As if he didn't know. As if it mattered whether it was the water pump or the brakes or a broken hose or... He was furious. Furious she'd taken chances with her life. When he'd told her to get the truck fixed.

"I don't know. The motor was making a terrible grinding noise. It got louder and louder and then I couldn't steer...."

"The brakes," he demanded. "Did the brakes work?"

"Yes."

"Thank God." His anger disappeared in a flood of relief. "And you're okay?" He brushed a smudge of dirt from her cheek.

"I'm fine. How did you know where I was?"

"I was at Willa Mae's party. Your aunt said you were supposed to be at the party. I had a feeling. Why didn't you tell me you'd moved?"

''I haven't had a chance. I never see you,'' she explained.

''You know where I live,'' he said wryly.

''I can't stop on my route. It's unprofessional.''

''I wouldn't want to put your job in jeopardy,'' he said. ''But is there a rule against being friendly with the patrons?''

''I'll check,'' she said with a smile, ''with the handbook. In the meantime...''

He realized they'd been standing by the side of the road talking, and while there was nothing he'd rather do than talk to her and drink in the sight of her like a thirsty man who'd been stuck in the desert for a week, he needed to do something about her truck.

He called Scotty's Garage on his cell phone. The tow truck came and hooked her truck up. Brandon told the driver to tell Scotty to install a new muffler, water pump, brakes, have the valves adjusted and give it a complete tune-up.

Laura gasped. ''Wait a minute,'' she said. ''Tell Scotty to call me before he makes *any* repairs.''

''I'll handle this,'' Brandon said tersely. ''I should have done it before. I can't have you driving around in a poorly maintained truck with no phone.'' Her eyes widened with surprise as he continued. ''Don't fight me on this. Because I'll win. If you want to, you can consider it a loan, but this is how it's going to be. If someone else had come along today... If your brakes had failed... If I hadn't known where to look for you...'' His throat clogged with the images that passed in front of his eyes. Laura lying in a ditch, Laura smashed into the windshield... She had no idea how fragile she was. Or how much she meant to him. He didn't intend for her to know.

"No. I'm paying for it," she said. "I'm not going into debt over my truck, and I'm not reduced to charity. Not yet."

He shrugged. He wasn't going to stand there and argue. But he was going to pay for the repairs no matter how proud she was. "Now, where to? The party?" he asked.

"Uh...sure, I guess so. Only, I'm a mess. First I was fooling around under the hood, but I couldn't see anything wrong, so I went around the back to look at the muffler, which had backfired."

He took her back to the place she was staying, a small apartment over the garage on the Fleming ranch.

"This is it?" he asked, trying to sound neutral, trying not to sound surprised she would settle for something so humble. Feeling worse than ever that he was living in her house, occupying her ranch when she and Dylan so obviously belonged there.

"Yes. I was lucky to get it. And I don't know how long we can stay. They usually let their foreman live here, but he took off last week and they haven't found a new one."

He waited in the driveway while she went up to wash and change clothes, leaning against his car and surveying the surrounding property. The same purple mountains in the distance, today covered by clouds, the same fields surrounding the ranch house. But what a difference. Now he knew what the Realtor meant when he'd told Brandon he'd gotten the most beautiful ranch around.

The McIntyre ranch, as he realized it would always be called, no matter how long he lived there, had miles of trees planted as windbreaks. The house was designed not just for shelter, but to blend into the landscape, a cool house in summer, thanks to the thick walls, and a warm house in winter, with its southwestern exposure. A welcoming house with its wide veranda and its large picture windows. He hated to think of Laura and Dylan stuck living over somebody's garage. It wasn't fair. Of course she hadn't complained. She wouldn't. That's how she was.

When she came down, her face was scrubbed, her dark hair shone and she was wearing a long paisley skirt and a scoop-necked sweater.

He tried not to gape, but good Lord, she was lovely. Even with dirt on her face she was a knockout. He opened the car door quickly before he blurted something like "You look beautiful."

"Did you notice?" he asked. "There's a dark cloud hanging over the mountain. Right above the ranch. Isn't that where your great-grandfather's mine was?"

"Where we had our picnic?" She turned to look up toward the mountains. "Yes, that's it. It looks like a storm might be brewing up there."

"Will we feel it down here?" he asked.

"Not likely. We might get some rain, but there won't be much, not enough to dampen the ground. Which is just as well. We don't have the topsoil or vegetation to absorb much water in the high desert."

A flash of lightning lit the sky as they spoke.

"Wow," she said. "That's unusual."

He glanced at the sky, then back to her. "Where's Dylan today?" he asked.

"I took him to town earlier," she said. "He's going to hang out with a friend today. I dropped him and his bike off at my aunt's this morning. My truck was working fine. He was wolfing down a slice of sugar-cured ham and biscuits when I left. Imagine that. Dylan even asked to go to her house. What a change in him this summer. He used to complain about her cooking, her antiques—well, you name it, he complained about everything. But now he wants to go there. Maybe it's because he doesn't like it where we are now. Too far out of town, too far from his friends. He's growing up. I hope so. We don't have much in the way of family, so we must stay close to the ones we have.''

She gave him a quavery smile and he felt a surge of sympathy for her. Sympathy he was sure she'd reject. She'd say they were doing fine. That they were lucky to have an aunt at least and a place to stay. That Dylan would adjust. But he knew how hard it was for her to be uprooted, to move from place to place. He wanted to help her, but he didn't know how.

''I'm going to pick him up after the party,'' she said. ''Oh. I don't have a truck.'' She frowned and stared out the side window.

''I'll pick him up,'' he said.

''How?'' She swiveled around to look at his almost nonexistent back seat. ''You can't put a bike in this car.''

''I'll figure it out. Trust me.''

''I trust you,'' she said. ''That's not the problem. I don't want to have to rely on you. I want to be independent.''

''You are independent, but does that mean you can't accept help from a friend? What happened when my car broke down? Did I refuse to let you help me? Did I carry on about my independence being threatened? No, I let you drive me back and forth to the ranch. I even asked you to.''

''That was different. You can't come out here and pick me up every morning so I can go in and pick up the van and the mail and start my deliveries. ''

''Why not?''

''You just can't. I hardly know you.''

He pulled up in front of the post office and turned off the ignition. ''You hardly know me?'' he asked, dumbfounded. How could she say that when they'd been as intimate as two people could be? Did it really mean that little to her? Was that the reason she'd walked out on him that morning?

Laura was surprised to see his reaction. As if she'd slapped him. All she meant was she hardly knew him, compared to the people of Silverado who'd known her her whole life. She wanted to explain or apologize, but she didn't know how.

''This is not my day,'' she said with a loud sigh. ''I should really go home and—'' Home. She didn't have a home. She didn't have a home and she didn't have a way to get there if she did have a home. If she wasn't wearing high-heeled sandals she'd be tempted to walk back to the Fleming ranch, go back to bed and pull the covers over her head.

But McIntyres didn't shirk their responsibilities. It was her responsibility to at least put in an appearance at Willa Mae's party. Otherwise it would look like sour grapes. They'd say she didn't show up at the party because she didn't get the job. But she owed it to Willa Mae to officially say goodbye to her. She wanted people to think she was just as happy driving the mail truck all over the countryside. It was a chance to give the impression to everyone that they were perfectly happy to be renting from someone. To wipe the expressions of pity from everyone's face.

She knew it would hurt to see the apartment over the post office and know she couldn't have it. But she knew by now how to hide her feelings. She knew it would be awkward having to make small talk with the new postmaster, knowing he'd taken her job away from her. But it wasn't his fault she hadn't gotten the job.

So she went in and made small talk. She noticed that Brandon did, too. She noticed everything about him. His sharply creased khaki pants. Who on earth pressed them for him? His navy blue polo shirt that probably cost more than her entire wardrobe. His dark hair that was now longer and more casual than when she'd first seen him. She had an irrational desire to run her hand through it, push it off his forehead. She wondered what he'd do if she did.

She realized she was never so glad to see anyone as she had been to see him on the road. Just when she was feeling helpless and forlorn, stuck there in an old truck she couldn't afford to fix, and without any way to contact anyone, he'd shown up.

She didn't believe in waiting for a knight in shining armor. She believed that women should be strong and independent. But when she saw him standing there, she just wanted to throw herself into his arms and let him take care of her. Which he'd done. The only problem was that she was greedy. She wanted more from him. She wanted him to want her as much as she wanted him. And she wanted to do something for him in return.

He looked so different from when he'd first arrived, with his granite jaw and his steel-gray eyes. Oh, his jaw was still firm and his eyes were still gray, but his face was suntanned, his eyes no longer steely. The lines in his forehead had relaxed; he'd even smiled. She wanted to make those worry lines disappear. To make him laugh. To make him realize that there was life for him after the death of his loved ones.

He'd come a long way already. Just like Dylan, he'd made progress this summer. But what about her? Had she really changed? The bitterness she'd felt toward Jason had melted away. But was she ready to take another chance on love? If she was, there was only one person she'd consider.

She watched Brandon talking to her aunt and David in the corner, looking relaxed and almost as comfortable as if he'd lived here all his life. Gone was the lonely hermit who'd practically chased her off the property the day he'd arrived. Yes, he'd changed, but had he changed enough?

Her aunt caught her eye and winked at her from across the room as if she knew what she was thinking. Perhaps she did. Aunt Emily had always had the gift of clairvoyance.

Willa Mae was the ultimate hostess, handing Laura a cracker with a dab of cheese on it and a glass of punch she'd spiked with champagne.

"If I'd known how much fun farewell parties are, I'd have had one years ago," she said, her eyes twinkling behind her new azure blue contact lenses.

"You've certainly outdone yourself today," Laura said, tearing her eyes from Brandon and focussing or her hostess. "I think everyone in town must be here. We're going to miss you."

"I was afraid you weren't going to make it," Willa Mae said.

"My truck broke down," Laura said. "Fortunately Brandon happened by and rescued me."

"That man," Willa Mae said. "He's rich, good-looking and nice, too. I swear, if I was fifty years younger, I'd set my cap for him. If I had a cap, that is."

Laura smiled. "Maybe it's not too late. Not too late to get a cap or set it. Maybe he likes older women. Not that you're old...."

"Maybe if I'd met him thirty years ago," Willa mused.

"Then he would have been about five, wouldn't he?" Laura asked.

Willa Mae chuckled and patted Laura on the shoulder. "I'm just kidding. We all know who would be perfect for him."

"We do?" Laura asked.

"I only had to mention that you hadn't arrived at the party and he went off like a shot. He was worried about you. By the way, I hope everything worked out on the Fourth of July. I felt terrible about letting you down that way. After I'd promised to put you up."

"Everything worked out fine," Laura said as coolly and calmly as she could. It wouldn't do to blush or stutter in front of Willa Mae. The woman had been known to meddle in more than one life while she was postmistress, shamelessly reading post cards and spreading news or starting rumors. "I hope your sister had a nice time in Silverado."

"My sister? Oh, yes, my sister," Willa Mae said, snapping her fingers. "Just because I'm moving in with her in Reno, she assumes she can just drop in on me anytime. What can I say? Blood is thicker than water, you know. Let me get you a glass of apricot brandy.''

''Did she enjoy the fireworks?'' Laura asked, amused at Willa Mae's attempt to change the subject, wondering if the ex-postmistress was devious enough to have plotted the whole thing. ''Your sister, I mean, the one from California.''

''You never know with her,'' Willa Mae said vaguely. ''She's hard to please. Where did you say you'd spent the night then?''

''I didn't say,'' Laura said.

''Smart girl. Speaking of fireworks, take a look out the window. There's a storm brewing in the mountains up above your ranch—I mean—''

''*His* ranch. I know what you mean,'' Laura said. She wasn't the only one who had a hard time adjusting to the ranch changing hands.

''Looks like Mother Nature is putting on a show for my guests,'' Willa Mae said. ''A kind of spectacular farewell, wouldn't you say? Excuse me. More guests at the door.''

Laura went to the window where a small crowd, including Brandon and her aunt, had gathered to listen to the muffled sounds of thunder and gaze up at the streaks of lightning over the peak behind the ranch.

''Good thing your dad build the dam and the reservoir,'' Aunt Emily said. ''Put an end to any threat of flooding on the ranch once and for all. Otherwise I'd be mightly nervous.'' Her aunt gave a little shiver and Laura noticed David Ray patted her shoulder comfortingly.

"I'm not too old to remember one stormy night your mother called and said they were evacuating. You were just a baby. You and your mom spent the night with me while your dad was out on his tractor all night channeling the water away from the house. After that, he built the dam. And there's never been a problem since."

Brandon listened to her story while he watched the clouds move closer to town. Although it was only five-thirty, it was already dark outside. He was a stranger there, and he'd never seen a flash flood or knew anything about building dams, but he was worried. He hated to tear Laura away from the party, he hated to tear himself away from her. But he couldn't stay there any longer and watch the storm hover over the mountain so close to his ranch. Just as he was about to excuse himself, the phone rang.

When Willa Mae came back from the kitchen, her face was pale and her eye were wide.

"Brandon," she said. "That was Bart Foster, the rancher out by your place. He says he heard a deafening roar coming from the mountain. He thinks it might be a landslide and the stream's overflowing."

Chapter Eleven

The room was silent for a moment, then everyone started talking at once.

"I'm on my way," Brandon said to Laura. He turned to speak to her aunt from the open door. "Would you take Laura and Dylan home?" he asked.

Laura looked like she'd been struck by lightening herself. "I'm coming with you," she said.

"No, you're not," he said. "There's nothing you can do."

"It's my ranch," she said.

He shook his head. "No, it isn't."

His words cut her to the quick. He could tell by the way her face fell, but at that moment it was more important to keep her away from any misplaced sense of obligation to the house or to the land. He had no idea what he was going to do. He just knew he was going to do whatever he could to protect the house and the land, and if there was danger, she was going to be as far from it as possible.

"If it's a landslide, you'll need your tractor to move dirt and divert the stream," David said.

"We don't have a tractor," Laura said, her lower lip trembling. "Not anymore."

"Bart has one," someone said.

"Let's go," someone else said.

There was a rush toward the door. A man Brandon had just met at the party insisted Brandon leave his car in town and they'd take his truck. Other men followed and they caravaned out to the ranch, staying in touch by CB radio.

"Never seen such a storm."

"Came up mighty fast."

"If it is a landslide..."

"Gonna need all the help we can get."

"Call the Fairleys."

"That reservoir can only hold so much."

"What about the dam?"

The question went unanswered.

Brandon could only imagine what would happen if the reservoir overflowed and the dam broke. The house could be washed away. The house that held all Laura's memories. He couldn't bear for her to lose that along with everything else.

The more the men discussed the strategy for dealing with the potential catastrophe, the more impressed Brandon was with the camaraderie and the team effort that was going into it. He'd never experienced anything like it. It was his house, his land, but every one of them was putting his heart and soul into saving it.

When they reached the ranch, Bart was there with his tractor in the pouring rain. So was another neighbor Brandon had never met. He was a stranger, yet the man was ready to risk his equipment and maybe even his life to help his neighbor. Brandon wondered if he would have done the same.

"Here's the plan," Bart shouted over the thunder, which rolled overhead, to the men who were dressed for a farewell party, not a rescue operation. "We take the tractors on the trail up to the reservoir, use our front loaders to cut a channel between the reservoir and the streambed. That forces the water to flow out of the reservoir so it won't overflow."

"If it does," a man named Joe muttered, "we've got a big problem on our hands. There goes the house."

LAURA GNAWED on her thumbnail all the way to Terry's house to pick up Dylan. Storms, floods, thunder and lightening. She'd never been afraid of them. Why should she? They happened to other people in other places. They were safe in their valley. Silverado had been there for over one hundred years. It would be there for another hundred. So would the ranch. Even though it wasn't hers any longer, it would always be a part of her consciousness. A part of her history. A part of her heart.

Dylan's friend Terry came to the door of the brightly lighted living room. The television set was booming in the background. A group of boys were eating popcorn and watching an action video. "He left, Mrs. McIntyre," Terry said. "We were all talking about the storm and he said he had to get to the ranch and get something he left in the tree house before it got wet."

Laura's heart stopped beating for what felt like minutes. "What? How did he...? When...? Is your mother here?'' She couldn't believe an adult would have let him go out in the storm on his bike.

''Nope. She's down at the church setting up for the potluck tonight. 'Case the power goes out, folks'll have a place to go. The babysitter's in the kitchen making macaroni for us. Maybe Dylan...''

''Okay,'' she said, pressing her hand against her heart. She raced back to David's car where her aunt and David were waiting for her.

''He's gone to the ranch. I've got to go,'' she said breathlessly.

''The road's flooded. We just heard,'' David said. ''You'd need four-wheel drive. And even then...''

''My truck,'' she said, blinking back the tears. ''It's broken.''

''Can you call Brandon at the ranch?'' her aunt asked. ''Tell him to look out for Dylan.''

''Brandon wouldn't be in the house,'' David answered. ''And if he was, the lines are probably out.''

''He has a cell phone,'' Laura said. ''He gave me his number.'' If she could only remember it. Her mind was spinning. Her throat was so dry she could barely speak. While she was thinking, David was driving them to her aunt's bed-and-breakfast. They dodged the raindrops and ran up to the house. Her mind cleared and she punched in the numbers.

Brandon answered, but his voice faded in and out.

''Dylan went to the ranch,'' she shouted. ''He might be in the tree house.''

''What?''

She repeated it.

''Okay...do it...worry.'' His voice broke apart. She set the phone down and buried her face in her hands. She didn't know what he'd meant to say or if he'd really heard her or not.

"I've got to get out there," she said, jumping up to pace back and forth in front of the window. "How am I going to get out there?"

"Laura, you can't go," her aunt said. "You don't have a vehicle, and even if you did… Don't you see you'd just endanger yourself along with Dylan? Then they'd have to send two rescue parties."

"But what if Brandon didn't hear me? What if Dylan didn't make it to the ranch? What if he's on the road somewhere and the water's rising…?" Her voice shook.

"He heard you. He'll find Dylan, I know he will," her aunt said. Then she put her arm around Laura's shoulders and led her to the couch while she signaled something to David.

He went to the kitchen and returned with three cups of coffee laced with Irish whiskey.

In the midst of her anguish and uncertainty Laura noticed in one part of her brain that David was very much at home in her aunt's house. So much so, he was playing the host, even starting a fire in the fireplace while her aunt comforted her. The three of them sat side by side on the couch, sipping their strong coffee and staring into the flames. Laura didn't know what she would have done without them. Just sitting there, listening to the rain on the roof with them on either side of her was some kind of comfort. If only she didn't keep visualizing Dylan, somewhere out there, alone and in danger. *Please, Brandon, find him. Find my little boy.*

DYLAN PUMPED the pedals of his bike as hard as he could, but he felt like he wasn't moving at all. He'd ridden from town to the ranch so many times, but he'd never had to fight the wind and the rain at the same time. Even as he pushed forward, the wind pushed him back. His rain-soaked T-shirt and jeans clung to his skin. Rain dripped off his hair and into his eyes so he could hardly see. He had to get to the ranch. He had to.

He told his mom he knew his dad wasn't coming back for him, because that's what she thought. That's what she wanted to hear. Because she'd given up. But he hadn't. Deep down he kept hoping he'd come back. But ever since he'd left the note in the secret place that only him and his dad knew about, he was free to leave the place. He didn't have to stay there waiting. It was fun building the house with Brandon, but maybe his dad wouldn't like it. Maybe he'd be mad when he saw they'd used up his wood and stuff. All this time he'd been thinking that when his dad came and didn't find him there, he'd read the note and come and get him.

But if the note got wet, if the note dissolved in the rain, then how would his dad find him? He wouldn't.

His tires skidded on the wet pavement, and he decided to take a shortcut through the fenced range land to the ranch. He dragged his bike under the barbed wire, scraping a hole in his pants as he pulled himself and his bike through the mud.

He thought it would be faster, taking the shortcut, but he hadn't thought about the rocks and the thick, bushy sagebrush he'd have to ride through. It was so bumpy his head hurt, and his teeth chattered so loudly, his front tire refused to plow through the thick vegetation, he got off and walked his bike.

Maybe it wasn't such a good idea to take the shortcut, he thought. Maybe it wasn't such a good idea to come back to the ranch tonight. But what about the note? What about the rain?

The rain was coming down harder now, so hard, he couldn't see where he was going. The puddles were deeper, up to his knees. Maybe he should leave his bike here and come back tomorrow to get it. He propped it against a scrub oak tree and continued on toward the ranch. His legs felt like they weighed about fifty pounds each, and he couldn't tell if the drops flowing down his cheeks were rain or tears.

THE MEN HAD WORKED STEADILY, digging, piling rocks, working against time, working against the water, but they hadn't gotten there in time. The water had already been washing out of the reservoir, rushing so fast that it cascaded down the mountain toward the ranch. Brandon had watched it pass by, imagining it filling the valley, creeping up the front steps to the veranda, destroying the ranch that had had been home to the McIntyres for four generations. Until he came along.

While he'd stood there, shovel in hand, his shirt and pants plastered to his skin, the rain running off his forehead, Bart, his neighbor whom he'd never met before tonight had slapped him on the back.

"Don't give up," he'd said. "We've almost got it under control. We're gonna save your place for you."

Brandon had nodded and said a silent prayer. *Please save the ranch. Don't let it wash away. It means too much to them. It means too much to me.* Then his cell phone, still in his pocket, still working, had rung. It was Laura. Dylan was on his way to the ranch. He couldn't hear her very well. But he knew he had to find him.

"I'm going down to the ranch," he told Bart.

Bart frowned, told him not to go. The water was heading that way. It was too far. Too dangerous. Told him to wait.

But he couldn't wait. He turned and ran down the road. He stumbled. He fell on the rocks. He skidded on the slick trail. His shins were raw, his hands were bleeding. Aeons later he landed on ranch land, trudged across the range and waded through the knee-high water to the house.

"Dylan," he yelled, but his voice came out as a hoarse croak. "Dylan, where are you?"

Where would he be? Brandon knew the answer to that. If he was there at all, he'd be in the tree house. If he'd made it. He dragged himself through the water that was rising higher and higher even as he walked out to the tree house. He stood beneath the ladder and shouted the boy's name.

In the dark he made out a shadow in the branches above, a foot hanging over the edge. Thank God. Let him be all right. Let him be okay. He climbed the ladder and found the boy curled up, half inside the house, half on the small deck, and he thanked God he'd finished the tree house. Because now the water was swirling dangerously around the trunk of the tree. They'd have to stay in the tree house until the water went down or they were rescued.

Brandon pulled him into the house, lifted the boy's head and looked at his face. His eyes were closed and he was breathing unevenly. "Dylan," he said, cradling his head with his hands. "Are you okay?"

Dylan moaned. ''Dad?'' he said.

Brandon's heart contracted. ''No, it's me, Brandon.''

''Where's my dad?'' he mumbled.

How was he supposed to answer that one? How was he supposed to tell him once again his dad wasn't coming back.

Brandon pulled Dylan's wet shirt off his back and took his own off, too. Then he held the boy tight against him, warming him with his body, talking to him, telling him everything was going to be all right. That the men were diverting the stream, saving the ranch and in the morning everything would be okay. Back to normal. He didn't say it, but that didn't include the return of his father.

Brandon reached for his cell phone and called the bed-and-breakfast. His battery was almost dead, her voice was faint, but when Laura answered he told her Dylan was safe in the tree house with him. He thought she heard him, but he wasn't sure. He shifted so Dylan's head was resting on his shoulder and they both drifted into an uneasy sleep.

When the sun rose over the mountains, everything was far from normal. There was water standing everywhere. But it was only a few feet deep now. Debris carried from the mountains studded the landscape. From their perch Brandon surveyed the disaster. The house was still there. He could see water lapping at the front steps and he heard a voice in the distance. A very familiar voice. A worried voice.

''Dylan,'' he said, gently shaking the boy. ''Wake up. I think your mom is here.''

Dylan opened his eyes and looked at Brandon.

"You came and got me," he said, his eyes wide. "You saved me. I knew you would."

Brandon's heart sank. The boy was confused. He thought he was his father.

"It's me, Brandon," he said.

"I know. We spent the night in the tree house. I always wanted to do that. You know what? I dreamed you were my dad. That's funny, isn't it?" He grinned at Brandon as if they'd planned the whole thing as a lark. An overnight in the tree house. As if there hadn't been a storm, as if he hadn't almost been swept away by rising water. Ah, the resilience of youth.

Dylan looked around, one eye bloodshot, the other swollen. "Hey, you finished the tree house."

Brandon nodded. "Do you like it?"

Dylan ran his hand over the smooth boards. "Cool," he said. And Brandon knew he was going to be just fine.

LAURA WADED through the water to the tree house, her heart pounding. If Brandon hadn't called her, she would have been there last night, hell or high water. But he said they were okay. At least that's what she thought he said. Maybe it was interference. Or wishful thinking. In any case she'd notified the crew not to take any more risks.

"Dylan," she shouted.

When he leaned over the edge, his face was grimy and one eye was swollen half-shut. But he grinned at her and she was faint with relief.

"Hi, Mom. I spent the night in my tree house."

"Yes," she said weakly. "How was it?"

"Next time we're gonna bring our sleeping bags, aren't we, Brandon?"

Oh, no, she thought. This time he'd transferred his allegiance from his dad to Brandon. An almost equally unattainable father figure. Now she'd have to start all over again. *You can't go to the ranch. Except when you're invited. We'll have to move the tree house to...* Where would they move it? Well, for now her son was safe, and so was Brandon. They looked awful, wet and dirty, cuts and bruises everywhere. When they descended from the tree house, she opened her arms.

She hugged Dylan so fiercely and tightly, he begged for mercy.

"Let go, Mom."

She loosened her grip on him, but continued to hold on to his arms while he answered her questions.

"I came on my bike. Left it in the field out there." He waved in the direction of the rugged range land. "It was rainin' pretty bad."

She stared at him. He had no idea how worried she'd been. She still didn't know why he'd left town and gone there in the first place. That could wait. She didn't have the heart to scold him. Finally he wriggled out of her grasp and ran off to survey the damage to the ranch.

Brandon was waiting. She hugged him tightly and he, unlike Dylan, seemed willing to stay in her arms forever. He held her tight, her breasts pressed against his chest as if she were the one who'd been out in the storm all night. As if she'd been in danger instead of him. He tried to tell her about the dam and the reservoir and the men who'd saved the house, but first she wanted to hear how he'd found Dylan and how they'd survived the night.

When he'd finished talking, he pulled back and looked at her. "Hey, I've got to go in and change. I'm getting you wet."

She looked down at the damp shirt that clung to her breasts. "I deserve it after what I've done to you. Sprayed you with water, invaded your privacy, disrupted your life. I'll get Dylan and take him home. I've got my aunt's car."

He took her arm and they waded their way to the house. They stood there looking at the graceful eaves, the huge picture windows streaked with mud and at the front steps still under water.

"Thank God it wasn't washed away," she said. "I was afraid—"

"So was I. In fact, I made a deal with God last night. If he spared the house I'd ask you to move back."

Her mouth fell open in surprise. "Move back? I can't afford to move back. It's your house. I've already spent the money you paid me for it."

"Move in with me, both of you. The house is too big for me. You need a place to live. I need—I *want* you to live with me."

She gave a ragged sigh. She'd never been so tempted in her life. To come back home. To live with a man she loved. Yes, she admitted it. She'd fallen in love with the one man who'd never love her back. But that was her secret. It had to remain her secret.

He stood there looking so dirty and so beat and so absolutely awful, and she loved him so terribly. She knew if she moved back, Dylan would have a home and a tree house and a substitute dad. It was an incredibly generous offer and it made perfect sense, but…

"I can't do that," she said.

"Why not?" he asked, incredulous.

"Because I—you… I appreciate the offer. I really do, but it just wouldn't work. Us living together."

His mouth tightened. He regarded her with a mixture of sadness and resignation and disbelief.

"Okay," he said. "Have it your way. I thought it would work." He turned and walked up the sagging steps to the house without looking back at her. She'd hurt him. She knew that. But she didn't know how else to say it. She couldn't tell him that she couldn't live with him because she loved him. It wouldn't make sense to him.

She found Dylan floating a board in the standing water in front of the barn and took him home. He didn't want to go. She never dreamed it would be almost as hard to leave the ranch for good this time as it was the first time when they drove away in their truck. But it was. She kept her eyes resolutely on the road ahead instead of on the rearview mirror of her aunt's car.

She listened to Dylan talk about Brandon the way he'd once talked about his father. He finally explained why he'd gone back to the ranch. To save the note he'd left for his dad from getting wet and dissolving in the rain. Then he turned the paper over and read the other side out loud.

"'If I had a son I'd want him to be just like you.'"

Laura didn't speak. Neither did Dylan. For a long time.

"Does that mean he'd want me to be his son?" he asked, twisting the scrap of paper in his hands.

"He means he likes you. He thinks you're a wonderful boy. The kind anyone would want for a son. I'm sure glad you're *my* son."

"I'd like Brandon for a dad," he said casually as if it didn't really matter. But glancing at his face, she knew it did matter. A lot.

She took a deep breath. She didn't know what to say. Her heart hurt like someone had shot an arrow through it. They rode in silence back to their rented apartment.

BRANDON SPENT the next several days overseeing the cleanup and repairs to the house, the reservoir and the dam. There were workmen there from dawn till dusk every day. He worked alongside them. He needed something to do. Something that didn't require any thought. Something that was so strenuous, he didn't have the energy to think about Laura and her refusal to move in with him. Despite the crews that came to work on the ranch every day, he'd never felt more alone. It reminded him of the lesson he'd tried to teach Dylan about the difference between alone and lonely.

He couldn't understand why she didn't think moving back to the ranch wasn't a great plan. The idea of living with her seemed so right, he had convinced himself she'd agree. But she didn't. Obviously she didn't care about him the way he cared for her. She didn't love him the way he loved her. With every passing day he was more and more certain it was true.

He didn't know how or when it started. Maybe it was the first day he'd seen her in her truck with her forehead pressed against the steering wheel. Maybe it was during the fireworks or afterward when he knew that every night would be the Fourth of July if he spent it with her.

One night after the workers had gone home, and the chill in the air suggested that autumn was in full swing, he took a cardboard box from the closet, opened it and reached for the picture in a gold frame at the bottom of the box.

There they were. He and Jeanne and their baby, looking so happy, he could hardly stand to look at the photo. He brushed his thumb over the glass.

"I love you, Jeanne," he murmured. "You and the baby. I'll always love you. You know that. For a long time I wished I'd died with you in the crash. I didn't want to live without you. But now I want to live. Now I have a chance at happiness. One chance. I know I told you I'd never love anyone but you. If you'd lived, I never would have. But I'm in love with a wonderful woman. I don't think she loves me. Not yet, but I'm hoping. I'm going to ask her to marry me. I think you'd like her. I know you'd want me to be happy. That's the kind of person you were."

He turned the photo over and put it back in the box, then he closed the closet door. And felt like a huge weight had been lifted from his shoulders.

SCOTTY CALLED HIM from the garage a few days after that and said that Laura's truck was ready to be picked up. Brandon told him to send him the bill and to call Laura and tell her it was fixed.

After work she drove to the ranch in the truck. He was happy to hear how the motor hummed and how silent the muffler was. When she jumped out of the truck, her eyes blazing and her cheeks on fire, he met her in the driveway.

"How're the brakes working?" he asked.

"Fine. Just fine. Scotty says you're paying the bill for the truck. I told you I don't accept charity. How much do I owe you?" She riffled through her handbag looking for her checkbook, he supposed.

"I'll make a deal with you," he said.

She stopped riffling and narrowed her eyes. "What kind of a deal?"

"You let me buy you a new truck for a wedding present."

"A what? I'm not getting married," she said, looking at him like he'd just escaped from the loony bin.

"Let's say you did get married. Would you accept a new truck then?"

"This is ridiculous," she said. "Who would I marry?"

"Me."

"You?" Her eyes widened.

"Who else?" he asked. "We could have the wedding here." He gestured to the newly laid grass, the hydrangeas and the graceful ferns that lined the walkway. "I told the gardeners it had to be done by next week. But if that's not soon enough..." Suddenly he didn't think he could go through with it. She was still standing there staring at him as if in shock. As if she had no idea what he was talking about, and if she did, she wanted no part of it.

"Never mind," he said. "I thought if I planned it all out, if I didn't give you time to think up objections, maybe you'd fall for it. What I'm trying to tell you is that I'm in love with you. And I want to marry you. I don't expect you to love me. Not yet. Not yet. As you said, you hardly know me, but that's one way of getting to know someone."

"Yes, I guess it is," she said.

"You might think I'm doing this to get a ready-made family," he said. "I confess that's entered my mind. You know how much I've missed Dylan and how much I like him. But I've thought it over and I'd take you anyway, even on your own."

"Well, that's—that's good of you," she stammered. "But what about your wife, the love of your life, the one woman, the only woman for you?"

"I know. I said all that. And it was true at one time. But not anymore. I know if I'd been killed in the crash I'd want her to go on with her life and love again. I think she'd feel the same about me."

He paused. Why didn't she say something? Why didn't she smile or cry or laugh or something? Anything but stand there with her arms folded across her waist looking like she didn't know whether to run away or run into his arms. He feared the former and he wasn't betting on the latter.

"Well," he said, "I shouldn't have sprung it on you this way. Obviously you're going to need some time to think this over. I've been waiting days to ask you. It seems like weeks...months. So I guess I can wait five minutes more." But no longer. Not a second longer. Because if she said no, he didn't know what he'd do. Life didn't offer many chances like this. What if he'd said the wrong thing, what if he'd completely misread her.

After an eternity, she smiled. A beautiful smile that transformed her face. A smile that made his heart rate accelerate. That gave him reason to hope.

"Could we back up a minute?" Laura asked. Her mind was spinning. She'd heard the words but they hadn't sunk in. Or maybe she'd just imagined them because she wanted to hear them so very much.

"Whatever you want. We can back up a minute or a month, just tell me what you want to hear."

"That part about...did you say something about being in love with me?" Her face flushed. What if he hadn't? What if it was just a dream?

He nodded. His gaze met hers, sure and steady. "It's true. I don't know when it happened or how. But it did." He reached for her then and pulled her close, so close she could feel his heart beating in time to hers. "I can understand if you don't feel the same," he said, his lips brushing her ear. "As you know, I'm not the easiest person in the world to get along with. But I'm learning. You and Dylan, you've taught me a lot about patience..."

She turned her head and stopped him with a kiss. She couldn't believe it. He loved her. He wanted to marry her.

He put his arms around her and after a deep, profound kiss that sent waves of ecstasy through her body, he pulled back and gave her a slow, sexy smile.

"Is that a yes?" he asked.

"Yes, oh, yes." She flung herself into his arms and he swung her around. "Wait till Dylan hears he's getting a dad and a tree house."

"Wait a minute," he said, setting her down on the ground. "Are you doing this for Dylan?"

"I'm doing it for me. And you. And Dylan, yes," she said. "Are you?"

"Yes," he said. "Yes, yes and yes."

She kissed him again. "I love you, Brandon. I'm getting you and my house, the tree house and my herb garden."

"That's nothing," Brandon said. "I'm getting a family and a family tree that goes back four generations. Your great-grandfather found silver here, but I found love. You and Dylan are my treasure."

Epilogue

The whole town came to the wedding. On a brilliant fall day with cool breezes and warm sunshine, Aunt Emily gave the bride away. Everyone agreed Laura made a beautiful bride in her vintage gown that came from the historical society's collection of classic dresses. For something new, the bride wore her brilliant diamond wedding ring. Something borrowed was Willa Mae's garter. Willa Mae had been saving it for her own nuptials which hadn't yet occurred, but she was working on it. The something blue was—a sprig of lavender from the herb garden, which Laura tucked into her bodice.

The reception was in the house and on the lawn. Laura basked in the autumn sunshine and in the love she felt surrounding her. From friends, relatives and her new husband.

''I told you, didn't I?'' Willa Mae said, drawing Laura aside on the veranda. ''He was the best-looking man to hit this town. And I'll tell you something else. I made that whole thing up about my sister and the Fourth of July. I don't know where you stayed or what you did. I'm not going to ask you.

But I said to myself, 'Give them a chance and see what happens.'''

Laura laughed. ''Well, you see what happened.'' She opened her arms wide to symbolically embrace the ranch, the guests and life in general.

''Yes, I knew it. I just knew you two were destined for each other. You just needed a little help.''

''Thank you for the help, Willa Mae. We sure miss you around here. Tell me, is Reno everything you thought it would be?''

''It's pretty exciting, but I don't know. I miss my friends here. But what would I do if I came back?''

''I don't know. If you want to work, they still haven't found anyone to take my place on the delivery route.''

''Hmmm, sounds like a good way to meet people. Drop by to leave them their special deliveries. Yes, I might think about that. Well, I won't keep you. Here's your wedding present. Careful, it's fragile.''

Laura set the beautifully wrapped package, which looked suspiciously like a bottle of apricot brandy, on the gift table, then she went to seek out her groom.

When she found him, he was sitting in the tree house with Dylan, two pairs of legs dangling over the edge.

''Mom,'' Dylan called. ''Come on up. You can see everybody from up here.''

She looked down at the long skirt then up at the two people she loved most. ''Okay,'' she said. ''I'm on my way.'' Gathering the folds of her skirt in one hand, she took a deep breath, remembered not to look down and made her way slowly and carefully up the ladder.

Brandon reached out to pull her up. They moved aside and made room for her and her dress between them, and the three of them sat there looking down at the guests and the ranch.

"This isn't like a wedding," Dylan said. "It's more like a birthday for me, cuz you got me everything I wanted. My tree house and a dad. I just want one more thing."

Laura sighed. "What's that?" She braced herself for requests of a remote-controlled airplane or a ten-speed bike, all of which Brandon wouldn't hesitate to buy for him.

"A baby brother or a sister."

Laura turned her head and met Brandon's gaze. He smiled at her and she nodded, communicating without speaking. *Tell him. Let's tell him what the plan is.*

"What about one of each?" he asked Dylan.

His shouts of glee could be heard all over the ranch. It was hard to know who was happiest. Brandon, Dylan or Laura.

COMING NEXT MONTH

#837 THE BRIDE SAID, "I DID?" by Cathy Gillen Thacker
The Lockharts of Texas
Dani Lockhart didn't remember her marriage to Beau Chamberlain—and neither did he! They had to get their memories back, and doctor's orders were to spend every possible moment together. After all, their baby was going to want to know how its parents had fallen in love!

#838 THE HORSEMAN'S CONVENIENT WIFE by Mindy Neff
Bachelors of Shotgun Ridge
A rugged yet gentle horse whisperer, Stony Stratton could tame the wildest stallion, but he was no match for the fiery Texan who'd singled him out as a daddy-to-be. Eden Williams *had* to get pregnant, and taking the redhead to bed would be Stony's pleasure. There was just one thing he needed her to do first, and it involved walking down the aisle....

#839 THE GROOM CAME C.O.D. by Mollie Molay
Happily Wedded After
One high-tech mishap and suddenly the whole town thought that Melinda Carey was engaged to her high-school crush, Ben Howard. Instead of being furious, Ben suggested that they continue the charade for a while. But when the townspeople decided to push up the wedding date and send the "couple" on an intimate honeymoon, how long could they resist making the pretend situation oh-so-real?

#840 VIRGIN PROMISE by Kara Lennox
She'd always longed to be swept off her feet, and suddenly virginal Angela Capria got her wish! It was almost as if Vic Steadman knew exactly what she'd desired. Every touch, caress and whisper told her that she'd finally found her white knight—now Angela just needed to find out if Vic was interested in happily-ever-after.

Visit us at www.eHarlequin.com